Documentary Theatre and Performance

FORMS OF DRAMA

Forms of Drama meets the need for accessible, mid-length volumes that offer undergraduate readers authoritative guides to the distinct forms of global drama. From classical Greek tragedy to Chinese pear garden theatre, cabaret to *kathakali*, the series equips readers with models and methodologies for analysing a wide range of performance practices and engaging with these as 'craft'.

SERIES EDITOR: SIMON SHEPHERD

Badhai: Hijra-Khwaja Sira-Trans *Performance across Borders in South Asia*
978-1-3501-7453-5
Adnan Hossain, Claire Pamment and Jeff Roy

Cabaret
978-1-3501-4025-7
William Grange

Classical Greek Tragedy
978-1-3501-4456-9
Judith Fletcher

The Commedia dell'Arte
978-1-3501-4418-7
Domenico Pietropaolo

Kaṭṭaikkūttu: A Rural Theatre Tradition in South India
978-1-3502-3660-8
Hanne M. de Bruin

Korean Pansori as Voice Theatre: History, Theory, Practice
Chan E. Park
978-1-3501-7488-7

Liyuanxi – Chinese 'Pear Garden Theatre'
978-1-3501-5739-2
Josh Stenberg

Modern Tragedy
978-1-3501-3977-0
James Moran

Pageant
978-1-3501-4451-4
Joan FitzPatrick Dean

Romantic Comedy
978-1-3501-8337-7
Trevor R. Griffiths

Satire
978-1-3501-4007-3
Joel Schechter

Tragicomedy
978-1-3501-4430-9
Brean Hammond

Documentary Theatre and Performance

Andy Lavender

methuen | drama
LONDON • NEW YORK • OXFORD • NEW DELHI • SYDNEY

METHUEN DRAMA
Bloomsbury Publishing Plc
50 Bedford Square, London, WC1B 3DP, UK
1385 Broadway, New York, NY 10018, USA
29 Earlsfort Terrace, Dublin 2, Ireland

BLOOMSBURY, METHUEN DRAMA and the Methuen Drama logo are trademarks of Bloomsbury Publishing Plc

First published in Great Britain 2024

Copyright © Andy Lavender, 2024

Andy Lavender has asserted his right under the Copyright, Designs and Patents Act, 1988, to be identified as author of this work.

Series design by Charlotte Daniels

All rights reserved. No part of this publication may be reproduced or transmitted in any form or by any means, electronic or mechanical, including photocopying, recording, or any information storage or retrieval system, without prior permission in writing from the publishers.

Bloomsbury Publishing Plc does not have any control over, or responsibility for, any third-party websites referred to or in this book. All internet addresses given in this book were correct at the time of going to press. The author and publisher regret any inconvenience caused if addresses have changed or sites have ceased to exist, but can accept no responsibility for any such changes.

A catalogue record for this book is available from the British Library.

A catalog record for this book is available from the Library of Congress.

ISBN:	HB:	978-1-3501-3714-1
	PB:	978-1-3501-3713-4
	ePDF:	978-1-3501-3716-5
	eBook:	978-1-3501-3715-8

Series: Forms of Drama

Typeset by Integra Software Services Pvt. Ltd.
Printed and bound in Great Britain

To find out more about our authors and books visit www.bloomsbury.com and sign up for our newsletters.

CONTENTS

List of figures viii
Series preface x

1 Documentary theatre and performance: Tributaries, trajectories 1

2 Documentary, multimedia and artistic prisms for social situations: 1925, 1964 41

3 Verbatim Theatre, Documentary Theatre and contests for civic change: 1992, 1993, 1999 79

4 Mediations and representations – multiple perspectives and practices: 2008 to 2023 115

5 Coda 151

Notes 156
References 162
Index 173

FIGURES

1. Programme sheet, *Trotz alledem!* (*In Spite of Everything!*), by Felix Gasbarra and Erwin Piscator, directed by Erwin Piscator, Berlin, Grosses Schauspielhaus, 12 July 1925 55

2. Actress Anna Deavere Smith in a scene from the NY Shakespeare Festival production of the play *Fires in the Mirror* 85

3. Actress Anna Deavere Smith in a publicity shot from the one-person play *Twilight: Los Angeles, 1992* (New York) 92

4. A scene from *The Colour of Justice*, Tricycle Theatre, showing the layout of the courtroom 105

5. Three muezzins – (left to right) Hussein Gouda Hussein Bdawy, Abdelmoty Abdelsamia Ali Hindawy and Mansour Abdelsalam Mansour Namous – at their stations in *Radio Muezzin*, directed by Stefan Kaegi, presented by Rimini Protokoll 122

6. Sarah Koenig (left) and producer Dana Chivvis in the studio during the making of *Serial* 131

7 An installation within *Domo de Eŭropa Historio en Ekzilo* (*The House of European History in Exile*), conceived and realized by Thomas Bellinck, Festival de Marseille Mucem, Fort Saint-Jean (2013) 141

8 *El Muro* (*The Wall*), presented by Teatro de La Abadía and Tobacco Factory Theatres. The image is from the version of the production presented at Sala José Luis Alonso, Madrid, 2023. On screen (left to right): Igor Shugaleev, Mokhallad Rasem. On stage (left to right): Freddy Wiegand, Maite Jáuregui, Chumo Mata, Ksenia Guinea 145

9 (Left to right) Josephine Papke, TRVANIA, Ana Lucão, Melanelle B. C. Hémêfa and Lahya S. Aukongo, in a publicity shot for *Even at the Risk*, a Ballhaus Naunynstrasse production 148

SERIES PREFACE

The scope of this series is scripted aesthetic activity that works by means of personation.

Scripting is done in a wide variety of ways. It may, most obviously, be the more or less detailed written text familiar in the stage play of the Western tradition, which not only provides lines to be spoken but directions for speaking them. Or it may be a set of instructions, a structure or scenario, on the basis of which performers improvise, drawing as they do so, on an already learnt repertoire of routines and responses. Or there may be nothing written, just sets of rules, arrangements and even speeches orally handed down over time. The effectiveness of such unwritten scripting can be seen in the behaviour of audiences, who, without reading a script, have learnt how to conduct themselves appropriately at the different activities they attend. For one of the key things that the unwritten script specifies and assumes is the relationship between the various groups of participants, including the separation, or not, between doers and watchers.

What is scripted is specifically an aesthetic activity. That specification distinguishes drama from non-aesthetic activity using personation. Following the work of Erving Goffman in the mid-1950s, especially his book *The Presentation of Self in Everyday Life*, the social sciences have made us richly aware of the various ways in which human interactions are performed. Going shopping, for example, is a performance in that we present a version of ourselves in each encounter we make. We may indeed have changed our clothes before setting out. This, though, is a social performance.

The distinction between social performance and aesthetic activity is not clear-cut. The two sorts of practice overlap and mingle with one another. An activity may be more or less aesthetic, but the crucial distinguishing feature is the status of the aesthetic element. Going shopping may contain an aesthetic element – decisions about clothes and shoes to wear – but its purpose is not deliberately to make an aesthetic activity or to mark itself as different from everyday social life. The aesthetic element is not regarded as a general requirement. By contrast a courtroom trial may be seen as a social performance, in that it has an important social function, but it is at the same time extensively scripted, with prepared speeches, costumes and choreography. This scripted aesthetic element assists the social function in that it conveys a sense of more than everyday importance and authority to proceedings which can have a life-changing impact. Unlike the activity of going shopping the aesthetic element here is not optional. Derived from tradition it is a required component that gives the activity its specific identity.

It is defined as an activity in that, in a way different from a painting of Rembrandt's mother or a statue of Ramesses II, something is made to happen over time. And, unlike a symphony concert or firework display, that activity works by means of personation. Such personation may be done by imitating and interpreting – 'inhabiting' – other human beings, fictional or historical, and it may use the bodies of human performers or puppets. But it may also be done by a performer who produces a version of their own self, such as a stand-up comedian or court official on duty, or by a performer who, through doing the event, acquires a self with special status as with the *hijras* securing their sacredness by the ritual practice of *badhai*.

Some people prefer to call many of these sorts of scripted aesthetic events not drama but cultural performance. But there are problems with this. First, such labelling tends to keep in place an old-fashioned idea of Western scholarship that drama, with its origins in ancient Greece, is a specifically European 'high' art. Everything outside it is then potentially, and damagingly, consigned to a domain which may be neither 'art' nor 'high'. Instead the European stage play and its like can best be regarded as a subset of the general category, distinct from the rest in that two groups of people come together in order specifically to present and watch a story being acted out by imitating other persons and settings. Thus the performance of a stage play in this tradition consists of two levels of activity using personation: the interaction of audience and performers and the interaction between characters in a fictional story.

The second problem with the category of cultural performance is that it downplays the significance and persistence of script, in all its varieties. With its roots in the traditional behaviours and beliefs of a society script gives specific instructions for the form – the materials, the structure and sequence – of the aesthetic activity, the drama. So too, as we have noted, script defines the relationships between those who are present in different capacities at the event.

It is only by attending to what is scripted, to the form of the drama, that we can best analyse its functions and pleasures. At its most simple, analysis of form enables us to distinguish between different sorts of aesthetic activity. The masks used in *kathakali* look different from those used in *commedia dell'arte*. They are made of different materials, designs and colours. The roots of those differences lie in their separate cultural traditions and systems of living. For similar reasons the puppets of *karagoz* and *wayang* differ. But perhaps more importantly the attention to form provides a basis for exploring the operation and effects of a particular work. Those who regularly participate in and watch drama, of whatever sort, learn to recognize and remember the forms of what they see and hear. When one drama has family resemblances to another, in its organization and use of materials, structure and sequences, those who attend it develop expectations as to how it will – or indeed should – operate. It then becomes possible to specify how a particular work subverts, challenges or enhances these expectations.

Expectation doesn't only govern response to individual works, however. It can shape, indeed has shaped, assumptions about which dramas are worth studying. It is well established that Asia has ancient and rich dramatic traditions, from the Indian subcontinent to Japan, as does Europe, and these are studied with enthusiasm. But there is much less widespread activity, at least in Western universities, in relation to the traditions of, say, Africa, Latin America and the Middle East. Secondly, even within the recognized traditions, there are assumptions that some dramas are more 'artistic', or indeed more 'serious', 'higher' even, than others. Thus it may be assumed that *noh* or classical tragedy will require the sort of close attention to craft which is not necessary for mumming or *badhai*.

Both sets of assumptions here keep in place a system which allocates value. This series aims to counteract a discriminatory value system by ranging as widely as possible across world practices and by giving the same sort of attention to all the forms it features. Thus book-length studies of forms such as *al-halqa*, *hana keaka* and *ta'zieh* will appear in English for perhaps the first time. Those studies, just like those of *kathakali*, tragicomedy and the rest, will adopt the same basic approach. That approach consists of an historical overview of the development of a form combined with, indeed anchored in, detailed analysis of examples and case studies. One of the benefits of properly detailed analysis is that it can reveal the construction which gives a work the appearance of being serious, artistic and indeed 'high'.

What does that work of construction is script. This series is grounded in the idea that all forms of drama have script of some kind and that an understanding of drama, of any sort, has to include analysis of that script. In taking this approach books in this series again challenge an assumption which has in recent times governed the study of drama. Deriving from the supposed, but artificial, distinction between cultural performance and drama, many accounts of cultural performance ignore its scriptedness and assume that the proper way of studying it is simply to describe how its practitioners behave and what they make. This is useful enough, but to leave it at that is to produce something that looks like a form of lesser anthropology. The description of behaviours is only the first step in that it establishes what the script is. The next step is to analyse how the script and form work and how they create effect.

But it goes further than this. The close-up analyses of materials, structures and sequences – of scripted forms – show how they emerge from and connect deeply back into the modes of life and belief to which they are necessary. They tell us in short why, in any culture, the drama needs to be done. Thus by adopting the extended model of drama, and by approaching all dramas in the same way, the books in this series aim to tell us why, in all societies, the activities of scripted aesthetic personation – dramas – keep happening, and need to keep happening.

I am grateful, as always, to Mick Wallis for helping me to think through these issues. Any clumsiness or stupidity is entirely my own.

Simon Shepherd

1

Documentary theatre and performance: Tributaries, trajectories

We might see this book as navigating between two poles represented by the following statements by eminent documentary theatre practitioners. According to the German theatre director Erwin Piscator, writing in 1968, 'Reality is still the biggest theater' (cited in Favorini 1995: xviii). According to the Swiss theatre director Milo Rau, writing fifty years later in 2018, 'The aim is not to depict the real, but to make the representation itself real' (2018: 281). We look to real events for the stuff that matters. And/or: what matters is the extent to which our theatre is real.

The focus of this volume concerns documentary as a mode of mediated live performance – as distinct from, say, documentary in film, television or print (although, as we will see, these media are also relevant). The main thrust of its argument is that documentary as mediated performance took conventionalized shape during the 1920s, became (variously over the course of the twentieth century) a vehicle for protest, persuasion and different kinds of revelation, and moved into complicated negotiations of what people believed to be both true and real in the twenty-first century. Some longitudinal trajectories already begin to reveal themselves.

One concerns the notion of 'truth' in cultural production. Documentary is inherently, necessarily bound up with notions of fact. That's not to say that it will always be accurate, or even transparent – far from it. But at its heart there is a concern with relations between shaping forces and lived lives, actualities and actions, and the realities (and figurings of the Real) that underpin them. Documentary is about what happened and, sometimes, what's still happening. It's not too far-fetched to say that documentary's trade is with Truth, which makes it a compelling study for what it reveals about ethical and cultural positions on notions of verification, representation, value, authority and meaning at different historical moments.

This relates to another trajectory, to do with the technologies available to artists. There is a narrative, here, that runs alongside the history of media forms in Western culture across the long modern (long twentieth-century) period, from the advent of photography and then moving images to depict actualities as witnessed; to populist and popular interventions in canonical forms of entertainment, enabled by new adaptations of recording technologies; to the proliferation of performances of all sorts (and indeed of facts of all sorts) across overlapping media and social settings in a hybrid digital environment. As we shall see, documentary theatre productions draw heavily upon the prevailing new media of the day, and their strategies and effects are conditioned accordingly. To that end they are often 'multimedia' in form, and in many instances have innovated in the use of media and technologies in performance. Documentary theatre provides something of a journey through shifting aesthetic arrangements of performance and performance technologies over the course of a century or so.

A third category weaves through this longitudinal journey, which might be summed up in the question, 'What's the *matter*?' And this question cues us into one of the distinctions between documentary in print, on film and television and in the theatre. The matter of a documentary might be the growth of a national railway network, or the flora and fauna of a subtropical region, or (say) the migratory habits of a species of bird. These sorts of topic are most typically covered in books and on TV. Early documentary films concerning the arrival of the train at a platform, the departure of workers from a factory or the operations of the postal service helped shape precepts about documentary practices, to do with on-the-spot observation facilitated by new recording techniques (see Murray-Brown 2003). To take a celebrated latter-day example, David Attenborough's work for the BBC as presenter of many individual and serial-format programmes provides a ready example of closely observed documentaries focusing on the natural world and produced through technologically advanced filming techniques.[1] We don't expect to find this kind of content in documentary-based productions in theatre and live performance. Instead, in these spheres, documentary has usually had a close relationship to matters of social, civic and political tension, and we often find it appearing in the theatre at moments of social change, unrest and conflict. Documentary presents models for public discourse, whilst it also offers insights into private and personal experience and perspectives, all managed through artistic presentation. If documentary theatre and performance productions tend to be notably 'formal' in their arrangement – often arranged deliberately across storytelling (narration) and direct address (witnessing), for example – they also tend to be attuned to sociopolitical churn or crisis, and profoundly geared around sense-making.

This means that specific aspects of documentary theatre and performance open out into conceptual and strategic concerns – for example, to do with the relation between past and present, the place of lived experience (that of both the historical participant and the spectator), and the status of things that authenticate the work (which might be documents that detail events, witness testimony from those involved, or civic and legal proceedings that might draw on both). Some of these concerns regularly appear, although the way they appear might alter, for documentary tactics change over time. Aside from anything else, we will also be concerned with an artistic and political relation with time itself, for in its presentation to an audience, documentary always looks back, while it often projects a desire for how things might be different.

In keeping with the format of the *Forms of Drama* series in which this book appears, we will consider specific case studies in the chapters that follow (one in Chapter 2, three in Chapter 3 and five in Chapter 4 – I'll introduce these briefly below). This means that the book does not attempt to provide a synoptic account of documentary theatre through the ages, nor does it pay equal attention to the myriad forms and formats of documentary. That said, the case studies allow for larger themes and strategies to be represented through detailed discussion of concrete instances. To keep these broader considerations in play, we shall have an eye throughout on the following categories, insofar as they pertain to documentary theatre and performance.

Documenting

We shall consider the nature and status of the record of the event (situation, circumstance, action), and how the record contributes to and is managed by the play or production in question. We will in places consider the document as an artefact, and how the performance itself (definitively an artefact) becomes a new document, providing onward authentication of the experiences or perspectives with which it deals. We will necessarily be concerned with how situations and events are documented; how documents (situations, events) are interpreted; and how the new work – the performance that's presented to audiences – offers itself up for interpretation. To that end, documentary is always *epistemological* and *hermeneutic*, to do with structures of meaning: how things are known and how they are interpreted.

Time (history and presence)

Documentary takes place after the fact. It considers events that have taken place. It does so, typically, by accessing records – documents, recordings, statements – concerning the event at hand and equally by turning to lived experience. The latter is sometimes verified by other kinds of evidence (photographs, for example), or is conveyed to the spectator through a focus on the textures and effects of a situation for individuals caught up in it. Documentary performs a stitch in time: between reflection (looking back) and actualization (conjuring a moment). It therefore puts the spectator close to the moment and sometimes encourages a response that gets *caught up* in the moment (I think of spectators at Piscator's production of *In Spite of Everything!* – which we'll look at more closely in the next chapter – crying out when Karl Liebknecht is arrested). In one sense, this is a characteristic feature of realist theatre – it presents a scenario in the present tense, played out in the moment in which we watch it. The effects of this aesthetic mode, however, are foregrounded in documentary theatre, for we understand that whilst we witness this representation here and now, its subject *actually took place*, previously, in another here and now. Time is doubled and, in the process, intensified. This, too, is a reality effect. The 'this-is' for the spectator is additionally charged through being 'this-was' for others. In her consideration of re-enactments, Rebecca Schneider dwells on the phenomenal quality of time as both substrate and topic of performance: 'Touching time against itself, by bringing time *again and again* out of joint into theatrical, even anamorphic, relief presents the real, the actual, the raw and the true as, precisely, the zigzagging, diagonal, and crookedly imprecise returns of time' (2011: 16). Whilst this describes a certain sort of temporality in performance, it also applies to the organization of presence in documentary theatre. For if nothing else, documentary is geared around making 'the real, the actual, the raw and the true' appear.[2]

Revelation and intervention

I've presented these here as a pair, because so often in documentary they operate in close relation. If documentary is about showing and interpreting, it is therefore profoundly geared around revealing. Its project is to manifest things as they were, or are, and in doing so to bring to attention details that have been lost, or misunderstood, or simply require gathering. This project of assemblage typically arises from a determination to explain or expose a situation, recuperate a history, or shape a position – and in that sense, documentary often marks an intervention in a circumstance, whether to require a new understanding, insist upon remembrance, frame a lament or advocate for a course of action. Documentary frequently operates with and through civic discourse, transacting with public statements and processes in order to bring its own thought process – its own *sense-making* – into the public arena. This involves a politics of public presentation. What is the knowledge, who determines it, how is it instrumentalized, to what end, what is agreed as a consequence – what *happened* or *happens* as a consequence? Documentary is thereby notably public, not simply in that performances are presented in public (that's usually a given in the theatre), but because they concern matters of civic and socio-political organization. They also concern things that define or change people's lives and, in that respect, documentary often makes the private public – another feature of its revelatory tendency.

Theatres of the real/performances of truth

Documentary theatre and performance concerns itself with reflection upon actual situations, events and experiences. As such, documentary deals with specific settings and occasions, and with what happened and what was perceived in these instances. This means that documentary deals with versions of reality – whether or not it problematizes these, or asks the audience to reflect upon the way in which events have been interpreted (where there might be different interpretations). We will therefore be interested in documentary theatre's claims on reality – its own, but also the claims of the material that it presents. Closely connected to this, documentary theatre transacts supposed truths – sourced from its materials and posited in the moment of presentation. Inherently this raises questions concerning authenticity (to what extent the material, the experience, the facts accurately belong to a given reality); individual engagement (how people's situation helps explain their experience and perspective); and belief. And whilst – as we shall see – facts and the historical record are neither stable nor commonly agreed, this in turn opens into the yet more unstable terrain of irony, untrustworthiness and deliberate faking. In any case, documentary theatre and performance are always concerned with situations of representation: events and experiences are re-presented, so that (through their mediation) they can be understood for what they are – or, we should rather say, for what they appear to reveal of themselves through the sense-making mechanisms of the production.

Experience

Documentary might concern itself with phenomena in nature, or cosmology, but our focus in this volume is on documentary that deals with civic and social matters. As suggested above, there is always a public aspect to anything concerned with sociopolitical organization. This lands in lived experience, however, and documentary frequently concerns group and individual identities, examines how constructions of ethnicity, class or gender lie behind defining moments, and explores how events and actions impact upon individuals. It is important to say that 'experience' also wraps in the spectator, whose engagement with the performance or production is a key feature of the transactional nature of theatre (broadly) and documentary theatre's offer of revelation (more specifically). This engagement is affective and can produce feelings of affirmation, validation, incredulity and anger.

These overlapping categories percolate through this book. They will variously come into focus depending on the specific work in question. They provide something of a continuum beneath the chapters addressing our case studies; and they help us navigate questions about cultural production and relations between aesthetic organization, sociopolitical situation and individual engagement. To explore this further, let's start with the truth (and otherwise).

Documentary and truth

While in exile in Denmark (having left Germany in 1933 not long before his books were burned by the Nazis and his German citizenship renounced), Bertolt Brecht affixed a statement over his desk that said, 'Truth is concrete.' As Florian Malzacher observes, 'In a time of extreme political turbulence, it was a constant reminder never to forget the reality around him' (Malzacher 2015: 5). It was also a statement of ontological certainty. Real actions have real effects and these can be identified and analysed.

Would Brecht be able to say the same today? Perhaps he would; and even more assuredly, if the levels of commitment to truth-claims by (for example) supporters of QAnon are anything to go by. QAnon is the umbrella term for both a group of people posting on the internet and the wider tenor of assertions that they post, geared around an overarching conspiracy theory that a group of satanists have infiltrated and control the political and media establishment. Spurious truth-claims include that the 2020 US presidential election was 'stolen'; and that leaders of the Democrat opposition cannibalize innocent children (see Roose 2021). This might sound extreme, but Roose notes that in a poll conducted in December 2021 'NPR and Ipsos found that 17 percent of Americans believed that the core falsehood of QAnon – that "a group of Satan-worshiping elites who run a child sex ring are trying to control our politics and media" – was true' (Roose 2021). This cues us into the dissonance of the notion of truth in a post-industrial, post-postmodern culture. Perhaps Brecht would have struggled, after all. Cultural commentators now widely agree that truth appears to be anything but concrete.

Kelsey Jacobson provides a good example. In her book *Real-ish*, Jacobson suggests that 'from truthiness to deepfakes, and QAnon to anti-vaxxers, the cultural touchstones of the past several years are emblematic of … a time in which the tenuousness of the perceptual border between what is real and what is fake has been laid bare' (2023: ix). Jacobson marshals some telling terminology from others who seek to depict what has happened. Vaccari and Chadwick, for example, describe 'a climate of indeterminacy about truth and falsity', while Rachel Botsman finds that this is a time of 'dispersed trust', where systems and institutions are viewed typically with suspicion (cited in Jacobson 2023: xi). In this extending cultural moment, Jacobson finds that 'what is real, truthful or factual is increasingly a question of subjective perception rather than an ontological certainty' (x). Hence her coinage of the term 'real-ish', in order to highlight 'perceptions, feelings, or qualifications of realness' (11).

Oxford Dictionaries selected 'post-truth' as word of the year in 2016, defined as an adjective 'relating to or denoting circumstances in which objective facts are less influential in shaping public opinion than appeals to emotion and personal belief' (see Flood 2016; McIntyre 2018: 1–15). The adjudicating panel expressly associated the term with the shocks provided by the outcome of the US presidential election at the end of 2015 and the Brexit referendum in the UK the following year (ibid.). 'Fake news' was Word of the Year for

Collins Dictionaries the following year, denoting 'false, often sensational, information disseminated under the guise of news reporting' (although the term is most associated with Donald Trump, who frequently mobilizes it in the face of factual reporting) (see Flood 2017). Both winning terms are not simply a single word, but compounds that denote a movement beyond epistemic stability and towards a domain in which statements and representations are not what they seem.

In his breezy and accessible book *Post-Truth*, philosopher Lee McIntyre reflects upon post-truth as a distinctly new phenomenon in contemporary culture and politics:

> Some may wonder whether the idea of post-truth is really all that new? Isn't it just synonymous with propaganda? … what is striking about the idea of post-truth is not just that truth is being challenged, *but that it is being challenged as a mechanism for asserting political dominance.*
>
> (2018: xiv, original emphasis)

This is a strategic matter, but one conducted through a discourse and political agency that have reset civic and social assumptions and practices. In which case, we are addressing a fundamental structural change. As McIntyre summarizes, 'post-truth is not so much a claim that truth *does not exist* as that *facts are subordinate to our political point of view*' (2018: 11; original emphasis).

There are various ways of scoping this erosion of certainty in the things people hold to be true. One is that this is an inexorable outcome of the longer effect of postmodernism, which undertook considerable work in decentring, relativizing and disputing authorities of various kinds. Postmodernism was fascinated by undecidability, and rather than establish undecidability as the prevailing cultural episteme, this laid the ground instead for plural decidability – a public sphere in which radical difference became a mainstream condition of political practice (see, for instance, McIntyre 2018: 123–50). Not entirely unrelated, consider the extension of a shifty form of corporate and cultural hegemony in a late-capitalist, highly mediatized public domain. For example, William C. Boles begins his edited volume *Theater in a Post-Truth World* by describing a meeting in New York on 15 December 1953 of heads of the major cigarette corporations. The gathering addressed recent research at the time that indicated a link between cigarettes and cancer. The response of the executives was to agree the establishment of the Tobacco Industry Research Committee (TIRC), to investigate the claims of scientists; and undertake a 'pro-cigarettes' public relations campaign that disseminated a positive message concerning smoking. As Boles says, 'This focus on "feelings" rather than "facts" would later become the core attribute of post-truth when it came to the forefront in 2016' (2022: para 8.5). Boles lists various campaigns that adopted similar tactics to defend positions that others would see as indefensible, including for instance those 'challenging guns and gun safety, climate change, issues surrounding health care, immigration reform, Voter ID laws, abortion, gay marriage, and many other political and professional hot topics' (para 8.16). The very nature of this list evokes a contemporary cocktail: the committed assertion or disputation of facts; the mediation of a message; and an appeal to visceral feelings of identity. In this scenario, an individual's belief makes something the case (to them), rather than objective evidence. Or perhaps better, we might say that an individual's affiliation (to an idea, an interest, an identity) produces the believable position.

This marks a sea change in ideas about cultural production relating to the real, and it strikes at the heart of the documentary project. Writing in 1990 Derek Paget (whose work we shall return to below) explains that he has capitalized 'True Stories' in his book on drama documentary since the 'true story' is a staple of drama in 'first-world culture' in the late-twentieth century (1990: 1). Paget suggests that '"the facts" have become a fetish in the twentieth century' (3). It seems that in the twenty-first century, we have instead fetishized feelings. This doesn't so much jeopardize documentary as amplify a zone of engagement precisely around ideas of actuality and countervailing indications of the inauthentic. Many writers on theatre and performance, for example, have noted both a turn to authenticity and a fascination with its erosion. This dual perspective was articulated with fresh vigour in performance studies early in the second decade of the twenty-first century (see, for example, Martin 2010; Schulze 2017).

To take one example here, Lib Taylor discusses authenticity in relation to two different approaches, exemplified by the work of Alecky Blythe and the Wooster Group. Blythe and her company Recorded Delivery's productions include *Come Out Eli* (2003), *Cruising* (2006), *The Girlfriend Experience* (2008) and *Do We Look Like Refugees* (2010).[3] The company developed a distinctive approach to staging in which the actors wear headphones or earpieces that relay the testimony of interviewees. The actors re-voice the original speech as accurately as possible in performance. As Taylor suggests, for Blythe 'It is fidelity to an original that legitimates and gives integrity to her performances, even if the audience are unaware of the process by which the performance is realised' (2013: 369). I'm not sure the audience is that unaware, but the point remains that the recording is occluded in the act of its reprise. Taylor also discusses *Poor Theatre* by the Wooster Group (first performed in 2003), which includes a section re-enacting part of Polish director Jerzy Grotowski's 1965 production of *Akropolis*. The task here is not to return the audience to the conditions and experience of spectators watching *Akropolis* for the first time, but rather to stage the trope of replication. For the Wooster Group, Taylor argues, 'authenticity lies in the integrity of a performance that reveals the artificiality of theatre ... While for Blythe, matching an original produces a truth, for the Wooster Group, imitation can only ever be simulation' (369).

This brings us back to the distinction with which I opened this chapter (exemplified in the statements by Piscator and Rau) – between a notion that the act of mediation returns us to an originary place or person, and the idea that mediation is always, in and of itself, an originary act (even while it is presenting a copy). Whilst in Taylor's account this appears to be a fork in the road, the decade since her article was published has demonstrated that even these dual perspectives on authenticity have become more complicated. In their book *Theatre of Real People*, for example, Garde and Mumford are at pains to emphasize that 'Our use of the phrase "Authenticity-Effects" is itself an endorsement of a sceptical approach towards the notion of direct contact with truthful, sincere or unmediated speech, selves, and bodies' (2016: 77). And yet, as the authors indicate, 'Authenticity-Effects' are among theatre's stock-in-trade (69–87). As Jacobson summarizes, 'Authenticity ... is less an ontological surety and more the result of a nuanced discursive or performative process that allows for interplay between multiple perceptual processes and multiple understandings of what is real' (2023: 7). Jacobson describes what has become a prevailing mode rather than an emergent trend.

Rabih Mroué, whose own performance pieces deal with challenging personal and political scenarios relating to his identity as a Lebanese artist, provides a nuanced perspective. He discusses artistic practice in Lebanon since the end of the Lebanese Civil War(s). Mroué describes an artistic strategy that turns to and fuses a variety of source materials, including 'hearsay, rumors, scandals, accusations, narratives, betrayals' (2015: 165) that are then organized in works that present complicated interrelations rather than simple single perspectives. There is a deliberate blending of reality and fiction in service of a critical and sometimes subversive gaze. As Mroué suggests:

> Certainly, these works of art are not intended to cheat or mislead their audience. Nor are they designed to trick or create the illusion of a truth. Rather, their foremost objective, from the moment their meanings begin to unfold is to place the spectator in a realm of interrogation, where he/she is invited to revisit 'established truths,' official narratives, and representations.
>
> (2015: 165)

The truth isn't always straightforward – and needn't be concrete. Rather, mobilizing a critical perspective is key. As I write this, nearly a quarter of the way through the twenty-first century, documentary in relation to performance is less to do with a specific artistic genre, and rather more with a widespread fascination with authenticity and inauthenticity within contemporary mediation – one that contains both authenticity effects and fabrication.

Documentary: tributaries and hinterlands

In her introductory essay to a special edition of *The Drama Review* addressing documentary theatre, Carol Martin suggests that this is a form 'in which technology is a primary factor in the transmission of knowledge ... Technology is often the initial generating component of the tripartite structure of contemporary documentary theatre: technology, text, and body' (2006: 9). Martin's discussion implies that we should also consider 'direction' as a fourth category, to denote the organization of material within a theatrical frame – an artistic meld of dramaturgy and mediation. Martin expands the notion of text to include the various archival resources of documentary, and points to Diana Taylor's influential distinction between the archive (an extant resource of products and artefacts) and the 'repertoire' (an embodied and experiential inhabiting of actuality – so also a resource for documentary practice) (Martin 2006: 10; see also Taylor 2003: 19–21). Martin acknowledges the 'aesthetic imaginaries' of documentary theatre (10) – which moves us from text, through mediation, to dramaturgy. The habits and possibilities that belong to this fourth category change through time just as much as technology changes. This means that we are interested in how artistic form, arrangements of space and action, and techniques of scenic presentation, change alongside (and often directly impelled by) shifts in what the available technology allows. Indeed, the history of documentary is also a history of the development of the theatrical apparatus, configured by new and emergent modes of scenography, technical realization and media interrelation.

If there were an origin story of twentieth-century documentary theatre (mindful of direction and technology), it would arguably have two tributaries: the first arises in the naturalist theatre practice of the late-nineteenth century in Europe, with its fixation on the appearance and revelation of contemporary realities; the second is expressed in documentary films, particularly those made in the United States and Europe in the 1920s, with their identical (but separately mediatic) fixation. Much has been written about both (see, for example, Pickering and Thompson 2013; Rebellato 2010; Winston 2019), so I will be brief here and consider two celebrated points of triangulation. Let's turn first to the work of the nineteenth-century French novelist and playwright Émile Zola.

Zola is interesting at least as much as a theorist of naturalism as an exponent of the form, by way of a set of critical pieces and polemics, including his essay 'The Experimental Novel' (1880) which argued for a form of experimentalism firmly rooted in new tactics for the depiction of reality; and the manifesto 'Naturalism in the Theatre' ([1881] 2010; see Zola 1893 for a collection of essays on new aesthetics). Zola argued for close observation and understanding of people as defined by their social, economic and geographic context. This is a matter of applying a scientific method (Zola turns particularly to the medical sciences) that is experimental insofar as it leads to new knowledge. There is a characteristically nineteenth-century confidence in epistemic possibility – scientist undertake experiments to arrive at findings (or 'certainties', as Zola describes them [1893: 9]). The writer should have the same focus. As Zola says in 'The Experimental Novel', 'It will often be but necessary for me to replace the word "doctor" by the word "novelist," to make my meaning clear and to give it the rigidity of a scientific truth' (1–2). The writer, then, should operate like a scientist to 'operate on the characters, the passions, on the human and social data ... Determinism dominates everything' (18; see Pickering and Thompson 2013: 15–26, for a discussion of Zola's idea in relation to the development of naturalism).

Zola's manifesto for a new form of theatre guided by these precepts is a call for an artistic revolution against the tired and outmoded forms of romantic drama and tragedy, with their emphasis on grandeur in storyline, acting style and staging effects. Naturalism – as a deliberately cool-eyed artistic practice – provides the answer, Zola argues, and the task is for the dramatic arts to catch up with other disciplines:

> the movement of inquiry and analysis, which is precisely the movement of the nineteenth century ... revolutionized all the sciences and arts and left dramatic art to one side ... [I]t has sent us back to the study of documents, to experience, made us realize that to start afresh we must first take things back to the beginning, become familiar with man and nature, verify what is.
>
> ([1881] 2010: 129)

This requires discipline-specific skills of the actor and the playwright (and we might say those of the director and designer, whose job titles had yet to be coined when Zola wrote his manifesto). Their task is to present characters who behave with psychological plausibility, in contemporary everyday settings, wearing the clothes of the day, and speaking dialogue that reflects actual speech rather than declamatory oration (135–7). For 'The future is with naturalism ... in the end we will see that everything meets in the real' (134)

Zola's novel *Thérèse Raquin* was published in 1867, and his play of the same name adapted for the stage in 1873. The play is not produced with quite the regularity of works by, say, Ibsen, Chekhov and even Strindberg, who extended the repertoire of naturalism in the theatre (while, as Rebellato observes, a wider hinterland of experimental theatre companies took the form by the scruff of the neck over the ensuing years [2010: 22]).

It does provide something of a template for subsequent realist playwriting, however. Zola articulated a comprehensive set of aesthetic strategies in the manifesto and set these in motion – at least in emergent form – in the playtext. As so often in naturalist dramas, the stage directions are copious and critical. After an initial description of the set '[a] large bedroom which also serves as dining room and parlour', and the various furniture and decor, Zola sets the scene for Act 1:

> *Eight o'clock on Thursday summer evening, after dinner. The table has not yet been cleared. The window is half open. There is a feeling of peace, of a sense of middle-class calm ... Camille is sitting in an armchair stage-right, stiffly posing for his portrait, wearing his Sunday best. Laurent is painting, standing at his easel in front of the window. Next to Laurent sits Thérèse, in a day-dream, her chin in her hand. Madame Raquin is finishing clearing the table.*
> (Zola [1873] 2010: 25–6)

So much information geared around facticity. The time of day, the time of year. A domestic setting with, even in these few lines, indicators of class. Details concerning what people are wearing, and how they are behaving. Lived lives, in what appears to be a very ordinary moment ('after dinner'). More, the evocation of ambience, to do with lighting (a summer's evening at the end of the day, the window half open), the reflective pose of one of the characters, and the authorial instruction that there is 'a feeling of peace'.[4]

Naturalist drama over subsequent decades would take these defining precepts – specificity of setting, attention to environment, the location of behaviour in relation to a particular space for living, the designation of specific class, ethnic, sexual and/or gender identity – as part of a template for theatre that depicted life as it is lived. Zola presents a schematic for realist representation that aligns with innumerable artistic endeavours thereafter to convince spectators that they are in the face of people, places and activity that have the appearance of being actual. This set of tools is of particular importance to documentary theatre-makers, concerned as they are with actuality – with situations of the real. This attention to specific sorts of detail is realized differently at different times, depending on the medium-specific tools available (a matter of technological affordance and artistic paradigm), and characterizes a much broader fascination with realist representation. To take two recent examples, we see this drive to accurate scenic depiction in the television series *The Mandalorian*, filmed with extensive virtual production effects created through the use of an LED screen that enabled actors, crew and the creative team to see performance in and against location in real time.[5] Meanwhile in works like *The Drowned Man* (2013), the theatre company Punchdrunk creates an environment for spectators to inhabit, where the invitation is precisely to savour (touch, rifle through, even smell) the props, fabrics, scenic items and arrangements intended to evoke a form of 'being there' in (in this case) Hollywood and its environs in the 1930s.[6] This takes us from Zola's insistence that naturalism could give its audiences access to reality, to more contemporary immersions into actual and virtual scenic space. While neither *Thérèse Raquin*, *The Mandalorian* or *The Drowned Man* are documentaries, they are part of its hinterland, playing out a rubric of realism that is derived from naturalist drama.

Writing in the 1880s, Zola helped formulate the precepts that provided documentary theatre with a ready resource for visiting and replaying actuality. Let's turn to a second tributary of twentieth-century documentary theatre – that provided by documentary films of the 1920s – and do so by way of two notable exemplars. *Nanook of the North*, directed by the America explorer Robert Flaherty and released in 1922, is one of the most celebrated and controversial early documentary films – not least since it raises questions concerning the ethics of representation and issues of cultural appropriation. A seemingly ethnographic account of the lifestyle and activities of the Inuit of the Ungava Peninsula in Eastern Canada, the film follows the eponymous Nanook (whose Inuit name was

Allakariallak) and what we take to be his family. At 79 minutes long, *Nanook of the North* is one of the first feature-length documentaries and became an international hit on its release.

Flaherty first travelled to the Ungava Peninsula area, on the east coast of the Hudson Bay, as part of Sir William Mackenzie's exploratory expedition from 1910 to 1916. In the text slides at the beginning of the film, he explains that he initially undertook some filming in 1913, having had no previous experience, and acquired more negative in order to capture more material whilst on the expedition. He then 'got out to civilisation along with my notes, maps and the films', only for the negative to catch fire after Flaherty had finished editing it in Toronto. Enough footage was salvaged to have at least something to show, and Flaherty concluded that 'if I were to take a single character and make him typify the Eskimos as I had known them so long and well, the results would be well worth while' (*Nanook of the North* 1922).[7] Flaherty travelled north again, he notes, 'this time solely to make a film. I took with me not only cameras, but apparatus to print and project my results as they were being made'. When Flaherty duly showed his rushes, 'Nanook and his crowd were completely won over.'

This appears to have all the hallmarks of early film documentary. Production is explicitly linked to exploration, and in turn positions both the film-maker and the spectator in a centred Western gaze observing the Other in circumstances that appear (to the gaze of the 'civilisation' to which Flaherty returns) remote and exotic. The text is itself a document of authorial inscription, providing a magisterial sheen of explanation and autonomy. There is a sense of Flaherty learning as he goes, an amateur wrangling new technology and acquiring proficiency, as a kind of heroic adventurer-technologist. The story of the burning negative reminds us of the challenges in handling film stock at the time, and Flaherty separately describes losing his film when his sledge fell into the water (see Rotha 1980: 39).

Rotha cites some of the critical response to the film. For Walker Evans, reflecting in 1953 upon first seeing the film thirty years previously, 'No one will ever forget the stunning freshness of Nanook of the North' (in Rotha 1980: 48). According to the critic Robert E. Sherwood in his round up of the films of 1923, Nanook 'was entirely original in form ... Here was drama rendered far more vital than any trumped-up drama could ever be by the fact that it was all *real*' (Rotha 1980: 48). And yet – we know now that the film was not quite as real as all that. The family were not an actual family, scenes were discussed before being set up and filmed, clothing was provided by a French fur company, and the family's igloo was built as a set with half of it missing in order to allow sufficient daylight for shooting (see McGrath 2007; Rothman 1997: 1–20).

One celebrated scene showed Nanook marvelling at Flaherty's phonograph – the record player that he had taken on his expedition, 'the white man's box in which singing and talking is so miraculously imprisoned' (as Flaherty's caption has it; Rotha 1980: 37). And yet, while this appears to be another instance of the explorer as gadget-handler, as Rotha observes, the caption 'contradicts even Flaherty's own writings on the sophisticated response of the Inuit to new technologies. Flaherty apparently relied on the Inuits' technical expertise to repair his photographic equipment' (37).

Nanook of the North exemplifies the tactics and attractions of the documentary mode; but also its dilemmas and dangers, concerning wilful or casual misrepresentation, the appropriation of other people's stories, and a potentially skewed relationship between situation, framing and reception. Although it is a film and not a theatre production, it is relevant here since it indicates how important photography, filming and recording were to documentary-making. The camera recorded people, landscapes and activities, and film screenings re-presented them so that spectators could see with their own eyes these other places and processes. The artistic rubric is iterative (we see the thing in front of us) and indexical (it appears to stand exactly for what it shows). Spectators over time became, in some instances, more attuned to the potentially misleading and indeed fabricated nature of such imagery, but in the early years of documentary film the appearance of reality meant that – to use Sherwood's enthusiastic term – the subject was more 'vital'.

A different example is provided by Dziga Vertov's film *Man with a Movie Camera*, which precisely celebrates this work of capturing the actual through the act of recording.[8] Vertov's film also starts with a series of text slides:

> ATTENTION VIEWERS: This film is an experiment in cinematic communication of real events Without the help of intertitles Without the help of a story Without the help of theatre This experimental work aims at creating a truly international language of cinema based on its absolute separation from the language of theatre and literature.
> (*Man with a Movie Camera*, 1929: 0:18–1:03)

What follows – shot in Kharkiv, Kyiv, Moscow and Odesa – has an almost intoxicating flow across a bravura array of topics and techniques. Calculated and closely observational, the film is also an impressionistic collage of shot formats and content. If you'll allow my own nearly random collation from different parts of the film, these include close-ups (a hand wearing a ring draped on a bedspread), a tilting camera showing a train at speed, a low shot from the front of the train of the track rushing towards us, a woman fixing her stocking and bra, shots of the camera being prepared, its handle turned to roll the film, a close-up of the camera lens, a shot of window blinds being opened, the camera aperture opening, the wide door of an aircraft hangar opening upwards, a shot from on high of the movement of vehicles and people, a street performer turning a mouse into a concertina (and the faces of children watching, in close-up), a shot putter, a person on an exercise bike, a line of dancers, women playing basketball. Shots within shots, overlaid multiple shots (for example of trams running in straight lines through the city; a typist and, fusing with her face, her keyboard), footage sped up; and in a delightful touch that is both metatheatrical and metacinematic, a shot of the cameraman on a travelling dolly, which cuts to a long shot inside an auditorium in which the movie is shown, the audience packed into their seats watching the shot of the moving cameraman on the cinema screen.

Vertov's film is a virtuosic, self-referential paean to modernity, the city, the camera and the very act of documenting. Observing might at times require a static camera and fixed focal length, but is anything but a static activity. Rather, it is an act of attention inherently accentuated through the framing work of the camera and fixed in the cinematic record. Films like *Nanook of the North* and *Moana* (1926; Flaherty's film about a Samoan community) provided the frisson of an encounter with otherwise little known or unknown people and places. Meanwhile a swathe of documentaries showing urban and rural life – including, for instance, Cavalcanti and Ruttman's *Berlin – Symphony of a Big City* (1927), as well as *Man with a Movie Camera* – presented settings and activities that cinema audiences were more familiar with but witnessed afresh through their mediation (see Hutchinson 2017 for a discussion of 'city symphony' films).

In Vertov's film the camera has additional status by virtue of itself being a subject – it literally appears in shot (filmed by another camera, of course – which reminds us that the camera has an also-inherent invisibility, but I'm concerned at this point with its evidential appearance). This trope – the *real-time presence* of the recording device, and its ability therefore to *mediate reality* – is a defining feature of twentieth-century documentary practice; and indicates a characteristic assumption of authority concerning recording practices across the board. 'Recording equals capture-of-the-actual' becomes a part of the cultural habitus. This applies to sound recording technologies, too, which had an accelerated effect in the 1920s and 1930s after the invention of the microphone (bear in mind that when Flaherty and Vertov made their films there was no locational sound recording that could be played in the cinema alongside the moving image). Around fifty years later, in the abstract to his influential article on verbatim theatre, Derek Paget notes that 'Quite simply, the form owes its present health and exciting potential to the flexibility and unobtrusiveness of the portable cassette recorder' (Paget 1987: 317).

The recording device provides special access for both artists and audiences. For a more recent example, and one that takes us back into the theatre, let's consider Katie Mitchell's phase of 'live cinema' productions, where staged action is also performed to camera (indeed *for* the camera) and relayed in real time on a screen above the live performance (see Fowler 2018; Ledger 2018). In productions like ... *some trace of her* (National Theatre, London, 2008), *The Yellow Wallpaper* (Schaubühne, Berlin, 2013), *Fraülein Julie* (Schaubühne, Berlin, 2013) and *A Sorrow Beyond Dreams: A Life Story* (Burgtheater, Vienna, 2014), Mitchell worked with her creative team and cast to develop carefully organized set-ups and sequences that would be properly legible only when played on the screen, while the audience in the theatre would also see the construction of the image within a realist stage setting (accompanied by a soundscape involving foley effects also created live). This requires a doubled attention from the spectator, who understands the relation of action within both the scenic theatrical space and the space of the cinematic frame. In Mitchell's production of *Waves* (2006), for instance, which Mitchell adapted from Virginia Woolf's novel *The Waves* (1931), members of the company work as both actors and camera operators, setting up camera positions, ensuring the correct framing of performers and scenic items arranged specifically for the shot, and performing actions designed to be particularly effective in close-up. (For an introductory video essay on Mitchell's live cinema, usefully illustrated with excerpts, see Davenport [2021].)

Whilst Mitchell's live cinema productions are not documentaries, they take on the rubric of documentary and the deep-seated guarantee of scrutiny and revelation provided through the medial presence of the camera. This instance from the twenty-first century sustains both tributaries I have sketched above and demonstrates a notable hinterland: the deployment of naturalist aesthetics in the theatre to depict both psychological and social phenomena, and the powerfully assertive paradigm of reality-capture associated with the camera and microphone.

Documentary theatre: phases, productions, positions

Let's briefly consider some landmark phases in documentary theatre and performance from around the 1920s to the 2020s and, in the process, touch base with some key scholarship and framings of the form.[9] In her book *Theatre of the Real*, Carol Martin suggests that 'there is an emerging consensus that theatre of the real includes documentary theatre, verbatim theatre, reality-based theatre, theatre-of-fact, theatre of witness, tribunal theatre, nonfiction theatre, restored villager performances, war and battle reenactments, and autobiographical theatre' (2013: 5). We come later to various of these forms and some definitions. The point here is that Martin's list – in a book that focuses mainly on late twentieth- and early twenty-first-century works – indicates what had become by then an extensive set of interconnected practices and outputs. It underscores Forsyth and Megson's assertion, in their volume *Get Real*, that there has been a 'remarkable mobilisation and proliferation of documentary forms across Western theatre cultures in the past two decades' (2009: 1). That timeframe, from the 1990s, marks both a revival of the form in some specific new manifestations, and the re-emergence of several continuities. To navigate backwards, we can do worse than visit the work of Derek Paget, whose writings on documentary theatre, television and radio have provided both historical and aesthetic frames of reference.

Paget is influential, not least, for defining 'verbatim theatre' as a going concern prior to its explosion in the 1990s and beyond. In an article published in 1987, Paget describes it as:

> a form of theatre firmly predicated upon the taping and subsequent transcription of interviews with 'ordinary' people, done in the context of research into a particular region, subject area, issue, event, or combination of these things. This primary source is then transformed into a text which is acted.
>
> (317)

Given that Paget also suggested that 'Songs are an important part of the dynamic of a verbatim show' (1987: 325) – which wouldn't be said now, nor very much from the 1990s onwards – we should note the shifting nature of 'verbatim' as a genre. 'Documentary theatre' is the term more readily used in US contexts, and Timothy Youker, writing in 2018, provides a post-hoc rationale.

> I prefer *documentary theatre* to such rival terms as *verbatim theatre*, *theatre of the real*, *theatre of fact*, or *testimonial theatre*, because *documentary theatre* emphasizes a shared engagement with the media of memory and a shared conviction that theatrical presentation of those media generates some kind of worthwhile intellectual, social, or aesthetic added value.
>
> (2018: 2; original emphasis)

Here as elsewhere, we are concerned with notions of time, the matter of documentary, and its tactical direction.[10] In 2009 Paget suggested a finesse to his previous definition, to the effect that 'In tribunal theatre, the "plays" are edited transcripts ("redactions") of trials, tribunals and public inquiries … In verbatim theatre, the "plays" are edited … interviews with individuals' (2009: 233). As Paget goes on to say, there are then formal differences in staging approaches, for example concerning the use of stage space and the nature of the actors' work. Paget addresses verbatim plays since the mid-1970s, looking particularly at Peter Cheeseman's productions at Victoria Theatre, Stoke on Trent, that used primary source material, including *Hands Up – For You the War Is Ended!* (1971, on the experiences of British soldiers returning from the Second World War); *Fight for Shelton Bar!* (1974, on an industrial dispute by steelworkers); and *Miner Dig the Coal* (1981, addressing the work of coalminers).[11] Paget discusses other shows, mostly in urban venues including the Gateway Theatre, Chester, the studio theatre at Birmingham Rep and the Crucible Theatre, Sheffield. He locates this work in a broader tradition of documentary theatre that has various confluences. These include the 'social document' work exemplified by the Mass-Observation social research organization (1937 to early 1950s), founded in 1937 by Tom Harrisson, Charles Madge and Humphrey Jennings. The Mass Observation team accumulated evidence concerning an 'anthropology of ourselves' by way of close observation of the everyday lives of people in Britain, captured by a panel of volunteer writers.[12] Paget also variously discusses John Grierson's work, along with colleagues in the British documentary film movement of 1930s and 1940s; radio ballads of the 1950s produced by the BBC Radio Features Department (which also point to work undertaken during the British folk revival over the middle of the twentieth century, including the recuperation of English folk songs and recording of local singers); and (the subject of his PhD) Joan Littlewood's Theatre Workshop in the 1950s and 1960s, marking a phase of post-war documentary theatre based on the experiences of 'ordinary' people, exemplified by *Oh What a Lovely War!* (1963, which indeed featured songs to excellent effect).

Subsequently, in *True Stories?* Paget discusses '[t]he rise of photo-journalism' across the first decades of the twentieth century, and particularly in the 1930s and 1940s, and 'the rise of documentary movements in film and radio from the late 1920s, and in television from the early 1950s' (1990: 32, 18).

True Stories? addresses documentary drama across radio, television and theatre, and in a subsequent work Paget focuses on drama documentary on British television, which became a significant form in the second half of the twentieth century (see Paget 1998). Let's note here the rise of reality TV in the 1980s which, as Claire Bishop suggests, 'has roots in a longer tradition of observational documentary, mock-documentary and performative documentary that emerged in the 1960s and '70s' (2012: 101; on reality TV see Hill 2005; on mockumentary see Roscoe and Hight 2001).

Meanwhile a US trajectory to documentary theatre includes the Federal Theatre Project (1935–39), funded under President Roosevelt's New Deal programme in the United States, which led to the inception of the Living Newspaper productions (see Paget 1990: 52–5). In parallel with this, oral history projects exemplified by Studs Terkel's ground-breaking work in the 1930s, collated in *Hard Times: An Oral History of the Great Depression* (Terkel 1970), brought previously marginalized or little-heard voices into public consciousness. I shall consider in the next chapter an example of documentary theatre work in Germany in the 1920s, directed by Erwin Piscator, which informs and connects with documentary practices more widely in Germany, Russia and the United States in the 1930s and 1940s, and resurfaces in Germany the 1960s. According to Thomas Irmer, this renewed German documentary theatre scene 'sacrificed the spectacle associated with early Piscator in favour of detailed analysis of documents, emphasis on accuracy, and the "responsibility of an individual protagonist"' (2006: 18). Irmer identifies the 1990s as a third main period of documentary theatre in Germany (after the 1920s and 1960s), featuring 'New forms of documentary based on auteur-directors' projects, critical of historical or sociological knowledge-making while exploring history as an open project that could not be known through accepted principles and ideas' (2006: 17). Irmer here refers to works by theatre-makers including Hans-Werner Kroesinger, Roland

Brus, Rimini Protokoll and Andres Veiel, now operating in the heart of a postmodern paradigm.

This brings us to a set of refractions of the documentary form in the 1990s and into the twenty-first century, although as ever there are roots in earlier work. For example, the prevalence of personal testimony in and through performance (in particular in feminist, educational and multicultural contexts from the late 1970s onwards) takes us into the territory of autobiographical performance, and onwards to the work of practitioners such as Orlan, Franko B and body artists who subject their own bodies to real time and actual distress and/or alteration – a particular sort of turn to authentic lived experience presented in the here and now of performance. In a different direction, verbatim theatre moved into the tribunal productions represented in this volume by the work of the Tricycle Theatre under Nick Kent (as I discuss in Chapter 3). *Half the Picture* (1993), the first production in the Tricycle's series, was composed by writer and journalist Richard Norton-Taylor, with John McGrath, from evidence to the Scott 'Arms to Iraq' judicial enquiry conducted by Sir Richard Scott, which examined the probity or otherwise of sales of military-related equipment to Iraq and the conduct of ministers amid the messy fusion of governmental geopolitical strategy and the conduct of business within tightly regulated protocols. It became the first play ever to be performed in the Houses of Parliament, and Norton-Taylor won the 1994 Freedom of Information Award for it. This marked the emergence of verbatim theatre as a means to condense and shed light on political process, its voices including those of the legislature, police and government. On the eve of the opening of *Justifying War* (2003; another Tricycle production, this time on the Hutton Inquiry into the decision to go to war in Iraq), Norton-Taylor observed that 'It was as if theatregoers were screaming for plays with strong contemporary resonance and political relevance' (2003).[13]

If this briefly represents the tribunal strand of work, celebrated (and widely discussed) verbatim plays include *The Laramie Project* (2000), conceived and directed by Moises

Kaufman, concerning the beating to death of a gay student in Wyoming; *The Exonerated* (2000), by Jessica Blank and Erik Jensen, which folded together legal proceedings and individual testimony concerning the stories of six death row inmates who were reprieved after their wrongful conviction was proven in court; *Talking to Terrorists* (2005), by Robin Soans, which gathers responses to terrorism by individuals involved and affected; and *The Girlfriend Experience* (2008), by Alecky Blythe, set in a brothel and relaying the perspectives of four prostitutes. The mainstreaming of the mode is perhaps indicated by David Hare's plays during this period. *The Permanent Way* (2003) explored Britain's rail network after privatization, specifically in relation to recent crashes, had a national tour and was broadcast on BBC Radio 3 on 14 March 2004; *Stuff Happens* (2004, National Theatre), addressed the invasion of Iraq the previous year; and *The Power of Yes* (2009, National Theatre), explored the global financial crisis of 2007 and 2008 (see, for example, Rees 2019: 262; see Luckhurst 2008 on a proliferation of 'verbatim theatre' in Europe and North America in the 1990s and the first decade of the twenty-first century, including a list of relevant plays [200]).

In many of these instances, verbatim techniques enabled a renewed 'political' theatre – and this is part of the direct lineage from the documentary theatre of the 1920s and 1960s – providing audiences with what appeared to be a fresher and more direct engagement with issues of the day than that of dramatic fiction. They also offered a differently granular account of lived experience; and they required a modal transposition of the relationship between director, writer, actor and text. The text was no longer the output of an originating author, subsequently interpreted by actors and directors; rather, the subject of the piece provided the originating voice (often literally), with the writer operating more as a curator and editor, and the performers in effect re-enacting rather than acting.

In the spheres of live art and performance art, the work of non-representational appearance – being yourself rather than pretending to be someone else – had long presented powerful templates outside the paradigm of character-based acting. Claire Bishop's writing on the 'social turn' in art practice maps how this tendency moved from the appearance of artists as themselves to the use of non-professionals as performers in contemporary art of the 1990s onwards. This trend, Bishop observes, 'stands in sharp contrast to a tradition of performance from the late 1960s and early 1970s in which work is undertaken by the artists themselves; think of Vito Acconci, Marina Abramović, Chris Burden, and Gina Pane' (Bishop 2012: 91). In contrast, Bishop describes what she calls '"delegated performance": the act of hiring nonprofessionals or specialists in other fields to undertake the job of being present and performing at a particular time and a particular place on behalf of the artist, and following his or her instructions' (91). Over the same period, various companies and artists adopted a similar approach in the theatre, including Blast Theory, Dries Verhoeven, She She Pop and (as I discuss in Chapter 4) Rimini Protokoll.

By this point, then, performance has incorporated elements that are notably from a realm of non-performance – an incursion of the real into (re)presentation, and part of a larger spread of documentary *presence*. I mean this loosely, to refer to an evidence base that can include people as well as texts and artefacts, that have the attraction of being self-evidently themselves (however much they are mediated and part of a matrix). One reflex of documentary, which plays out here (if obliquely, in non-documentary works), is that the actual ostensibly authenticates the performance/production. What does this mean for the document in documentary?

The document, knowledge and assemblage

Duška Radosavljević suggests that 'The documentary theatre of the twenty-first century is ... seen as being concerned with instability and loss of authority of the document itself'

(2013: 128). What *is* the document in this expanding scene? We might see it as part of a *dispositif* (apparatus), drawing on Foucault and Agamben. Agamben glosses Foucault's overview of the term (given in an interview in 1977) with regard to three main points: the apparatus is a network that includes various elements that intersect; it always relates to power dynamics; and 'it appears at the intersection of power relations and relations of knowledge' (2009: 3). In broad terms, this might apply to any document. Indeed, breadth in relation to the apparatus is part of the challenge of the concept. As Agamben suggests, 'I shall call an apparatus literally anything that has in some way the capacity to capture, orient, determine, intercept, model, control, or secure the gestures, behaviours, opinions, or discourses of living beings' (2009: 14). So, this can include all sorts of institutions and domains of practice, including prisons, schools, literature, agriculture – a very wide remit! That said, the document in documentary can easily be seen as part of a project of capture, determination and discourse. Perhaps the more useful aspect to this is Agamben's emphasis on subjectification – the apparatus works insofar as it designates subjects who experience themselves as a subject within the terms and protocols of the apparatus. As Agamben suggests, apparatuses 'must produce their subject' (11), while the apparatus is a 'machine of governance' because it produces subjectifications (20). I raise this not to suggest a common function (at least of subjectification) for documentary artefacts and practices, nor to suggest that documentary should be seen as a single apparatus – but because the work of documentary, necessarily within disciplinary and discursive frames, is typically to do with subjects (the documented, the documenter and the reader/spectator) in relation to circulations of power and an economy of knowledge. This expanded sense, I suggest, is a way of adjudicating documentary across its various shifts of mode, artistic strategy and indeed authority over time.

The transaction, then, is twofold: firstly, between what is already known, what is discovered in the document and what new knowledge is produced; and secondly, concerning which interests are served in this process of revelation. This is where documentary as a form has both reactionary and radical tendencies. I oversimplify, but for the sake of the juxtaposition: documentary is reactionary in perpetuating stereotypes and structures of dependency and marginalization; and radical in revealing situations that expose prevailing power dynamics and shape a perspective upon change. To this end, it matters less what kind of document we're addressing, and rather more what kind of tactic is at play in the documentary project.

So, for example, documentary performance doesn't necessarily privilege writing in its own epistemic drive, but rather the originary action or experience that is presented (through mediation) for analysis. What's shared, then, might be archival (sourced from documents from court cases, for example), or sourced from the 'repertoire' of embodied and ephemeral practice, to use Taylor's (2003) term. As we saw, Paget's finesse in 2009 of his 1987 definition of verbatim theatre marked a clearer distinction between theatre based on spoken testimony and theatre based on written proceedings. Nonetheless, the documented phenomenon, in both modes, is the spoken word; which might then be transcribed and subsequently edited, or might exist only as a sound file where, again, it might be edited. (See Schneider [2011: 99] for a discussion of an expanded understanding of what can be thought of as available documents, including speeches, images and 'ethnotexts' and see Taylor [2003] on artefacts and components that contribute to '"archival" memory' [19].)

If we think back to Dziga Vertov's *Man With a Movie Camera*, the documented phenomena are the city (including its fabric and architecture), the actions of individuals and groups within it, and specific objects in this setting. This is rather extensive, and the film itself becomes a primary document, as *an assemblage that undertakes the work of documenting*. In some instances – for example, the tribunal play *Half the Picture* – there is a documenting assemblage (the transcripts of court proceedings) that inform a subsequent documenting assemblage (the theatre production). This introduces another layer to the process of arriving at the performance artefact presented to an audience: a layering of the relationship between the originary actions or situations that are the subject of the documentary (in the case of the tribunal plays, these are both the tribunal proceedings and the precedent actions to which they refer) and the documentary artefact itself. This distinction – between an originary source and the documenting assemblage – is marked to a greater or lesser extent, depending on the nature of the project; but typically, the *distance* between source and assemblage is designed to be as small as possible. I mean this not in terms of timeframes (the documentary might be shared many years after the events that it deals with), but in relation to the experience of the spectator in an aesthetic and phenomenological frame. That's to say, the documentary aspires to immediacy of access. That's why documentary is so geared around reiteration – it necessarily revisits, in order to lie as close as possible to the originary scene.

Whilst this has always been part of the function of documentary, closeness to the real has taken a specific turn in arranged encounters that seek to put the individual inside something that has already taken place. In *Performing Remains*, Rebecca Schneider discusses theatrical re-enactment as a late-twentieth- and early-twenty-first-century phenomenon, noting that '[t]he practice of re-playing or redoing a precedent event, artwork, or act has exploded in performance-based art alongside the burgeoning of historical reenactment and "living history" in various history museums, theme parks, and preservation societies' (2011: 2). As Schneider makes clear in her analysis, this is a matter not just of fascination with historical processes (and, we might say, their productions), but a present-tense *embodied* engagement. She describes 'the replay of evidence (photographs, documents, archival remains) back across the body in gestic negotiation' (9). The document becomes an agent for corporeal action. In effect, this is a distinctive cultural shift from the auratic and non-reproducible (events and artworks existing in and of themselves, with a kind of precious uniqueness) to the recurrent and recuperable.

This might be expected as a cultural phenomenon in late capitalism, geared as it is to reliably repetitive production and serial consumption; and likewise as a function of cultural production in a mediatized scene familiar with the series and the repeat in entertainment formats. It also aligns with the technological underpinning of contemporary culture – recording, replay and retrieval have become dominant tropes, while the presence of the participant (as a player, commentator, social actor) is profoundly experiential. As Schneider says, of her own participatory encounters with re-enactments, 'I observed participants putting themselves *in the place of the past*' (9). Whilst this is sharply purposeful in re-enactments, it is also part of the prevailing function of documentary theatre.

And it's arguably this function that informs Duška Radosavljević's conjecture that 'relationality' is a key concept for understanding a broad range of performances in the twenty-first century, specifically through strategies for audience engagement that entail some longstanding precepts of political theatre alongside more participatory modes of contemporary live art practices (2013: 130). Radosavljević shares a list of different forms of contemporary documentary theatre within this broad rubric – and if we've visited some of them above, the outline usefully reminds of the scope of documentary including, as it does, works that are:

> variously concerned with written documents (Tricycle's tribunal plays), a literal transposition of words collected from real life (as in Anna Deavere Smith's work, the Russian 'orthodox' verbatim and Alecky Blythe's *Recorded Delivery*), facts on which dramatic events will be based (as in Polish 'paradocumentary'), 'the spirit' of real-life people being translated into the language of the stage (as in Out of Joint's work), real people themselves (as in Rimini Protokoll's work), or a combination of those (as in, for example, Philip Ralph's *Deep Cut*).
>
> (2013: 149, see also 130)

To this we can add the documentary inflection of social media after Web 2.0 (from around the turn of the millennium). Through online platforms such as Facebook, Instagram and Tik Tok, individuals curate their own lives, present details of their daily activity and real-time location, and in effect give witness and act as witnesses. Social media have reshaped how we understand the documenting of activity and events, and how commentary functions both from the inside of an experience and from outside in response to it. Social media platforms are more fluid, immediate and ephemeral than any previous mode of widely disseminated communication; arguably more subject to interpretation and misinterpretation than before, and in any case routinely subject to adjustment and editing in close to real time. That said, they also provide a more demotic kind of recording presence, which has been facilitated by organizations such as Amnesty International and The American Civil Liberties Union (ACLU) by way of phone applications that provide a repository for recordings of violent or oppressive behaviour by security forces (see Arjomand 2018: 172). And as Arjomand observes, 'Increasingly, cell phone footage of violent police encounters is live streamed, creating a live (virtual) public that witnesses the event through social media' (172–3). Such recordings have provided powerful evidence of police brutality that feeds into onward responses. Darnella Frazier, for example, filmed the murder of George Floyd on her phone in 2020, posting the video on Facebook and Instagram. Nearly thirty years previously, in 1991, George Holliday recorded the beating of Rodney King, his footage becoming a key piece of evidence in the trial of the policemen involved.

Documenting, in these cases, provided a basis for the massive socio-political developments in both instances. This is surely where reality meets the document(er). What follows is the stuff of history, but it is also, structurally, the stuff of the present moment. The modes of documentation – through technologies and dissemination suitable to the moment – are mobilized in contestations around justice, meaning and value.

Case studies

From the plethora of documentary theatre and performance productions, we turn to some specific instances in the chapters that follow. The case study central to Chapter 2 is *In Spite of Everything!* (1925), directed by Erwin Piscator and presented at the Grosses Schauspielhaus, Berlin, where it played to capacity audiences of 3,500 people. The original text is now lost, and all that remains is a 16-page synopsis. However, we know something about the principles of the piece, the process by which it was made, and its style and structure. The show was revue-like, presenting a version of the recent history of Germany from the inception of the First World War to the Spartacist uprising and assassination of its co-leader Karl Liebknecht in 1919. As Piscator explained, 'the whole performance was one huge montage of authentic speeches, articles, newspaper clippings, slogans, leaflets, photographs and films of the War and the Revolution' (cited in Mason 1977: 263–4).

In Spite of Everything! connects with the dynamic and innovative work of artists and theatre-makers in Europe in the 1920s and 1930s. It entails the incorporation of film into theatre events; the use of radically mixed modes of representation (mass spectacle, intimate domestic scenes, contemporary artefacts and items of record); a quest for what Piscator described as 'the absolute truth'; the mediating and shaping role of the director; the use of stage technology to present image, information and allow for dramatic and aesthetic 'attack'; and the idea of theatre as a public forum. We can look forward to Piscator's formulation of epic theatre in *The Political Theatre* (1929), and what might be termed a Brechtian seam to documentary theatre. And if we follow Piscator we can trace lines from Europe to the United States, and the 1920s to the 1960s. After a peripatetic exile he moved to New York in 1938, founding the Dramatic Workshop in the New School for Social Research – this allows us to catch up with the work of the Living Newspaper in the United States, and gesture towards a line of experimental performance exemplified by the Living Theatre, co-founded in 1947 by Judith Malina, who studied with Piscator at the New School. Meanwhile Piscator returned to Germany to become artistic director of the West Berlin Freie Volksbühne, where his productions included Peter Weiss's *The Investigation* (1965) – a re-enactment of the Frankfurt Auschwitz trials of 1963 to 1965. And Weiss takes us to the tribunal and testimony plays of the 1990s and 2000s.

Chapter 3 sets three case studies alongside each other: *Fires in the Mirror* (1992) and *Twilight: Los Angeles* (1993), both written and performed by Anna Deavere Smith in (respectively) New York City; and Los Angeles and *The Colour of Justice: The Stephen Lawrence Enquiry*, written by Richard Norton-Taylor and first presented at the Tricycle Theatre, London in 1999. They are taken together here to allow us to draw some parallels across and distinctions between two dominant scenes of documentary performance, those of the UK and United States. Each production uses 'verbatim' material, which was derived and theatricalized differently in the UK and US settings. They each address incidents and civil proceedings arising from acts of violence that provoked extensive public discussion of the state of policing, embedded racism (in the police, within society) and the inadequacy of legal process. The respective critical incidents led to lengthy series of investigations, which themselves variously contributed to changes in policing and the law. And it's not simply that the three productions provide a reasonably neat juxtaposition. They have a place in a longer story that's of profound significance to individuals and the social order. Documentary often stages the emotional and civic fissures in society – and some fissures are deeper than others. Each production highlights the endurance and the effects of racism. What documentary does, here, is something to do with *mattering* – and that in itself is to do with operating amid the wound of social values and cultural change.

The case studies in Chapter 4 take us from the renewal of documentary theatre in the 1990s to a hybrid multimedia environment that is arguably both post-truth and deeply invested in group and individual identity. What kind of documents, and what sorts of documentary, are adequate to this moment? This cultural scene is not easily represented, in this book, by a single case study. Since documentary has migrated into different sorts of artistic arrangement, I consider five works in this section, which together allow for discussion of an overlapping set of aesthetic procedures and cultural assumptions. These are *Radio Muezzin* (2008), conceived and directed by Stefan Kaegi of Rimini Protokoll; *Serial* (2014–18), a podcast by the American investigative journalist Sarah Koenig, produced for the radio programme *This American Life*; Thomas Bellinck's *Domo de Eŭropa Historio en Ekzilo (The House of European History in Exile)* (2013), a museum-like installation which Bellinck describes as a 'speculative documentary'; *The Wall* (2022), created by Juan Ayala and presented by Tobacco Factory Theatres and Fundación Teatro de La Abadía Madrid (2023), in which two performers whose lives are profoundly defined by the geopolitical circumstances of the countries they are from, participate in a live, remote encounter that is interpreted by performers onstage before a co-present audience; and *Even at the Risk* (2023), a show based on the spoken word featuring five women of colour who speak directly to the audience about their lives and experiences.

Our gathering ground in this chapter is the engagement of documentary performance with mediations and experiences of Islam, immigration, cultural change and Western identity. Beyond this, the case studies help to illustrate how the modes, techniques and assumptions of documentary bear upon narrative organization and the representation of specific communities and lived experience. They illustrate how artists use new communication technologies to gain information, present it and disseminate their work in often novel ways. They require an understanding of sophisticated processes of production; and continuities concerning the most basic and direct forms of theatrical communication. And they help elaborate on Janelle Reinelt's claim that 'The documentary is not in the object, but in the relationship between the object, its mediators (artists, historians, authors) and its audiences' (Reinelt 2009: 7).

Indeed, that's surely the case with all documentary outputs. Where to begin? The Dramaturg in Brecht's *Messingkauf Dialogues* says, 'I believe Piscator was the first person to think it necessary to provide *evidence* in the theatre. He projected authentic documents on to large screens' (Brecht 2014: 69; original emphasis). And that's not all. Let's turn, then, to this early instance of multimedia documentary theatre.

2

Documentary, multimedia and artistic prisms for social situations: 1925, 1964

In this chapter we focus on the production of *In Spite of Everything!* directed by Erwin Piscator at the Grosses Schauspielhaus, Berlin, in 1925. The show is one of the first key documentary theatre productions. Its place in this volume is due partly to its inaugural status, but rather more to its tactics for representing actual events, and its combination of elements including newsreel footage and as-if-verbatim scenes from historical incidents. These provide a theatrical exemplar for future productions and allow for some conceptual modelling of how this kind of documentary performance might work for its audience. *In Spite of Everything!* also enables us to trace a line through some significant documentary theatre practice by way of its director. Following Piscator, we shall travel through the political and theatrical ferment of Berlin in the 1920s, to the USSR and United States in the 1930s and 1940s and back to (West) Germany in the 1950s and 1960s – and a golden seam of reality-oriented theatre practice across continents and through the long middle of the twentieth century.

Piscator

Let's start briefly with Erwin Piscator himself, 'this fighting Humanist' as Brecht had it (in Ley-Piscator 1967: 290). Piscator was born in 1893 in Greifenstein-Ulm in Germany – not that far from Frankfurt, where about a century later Hans-Thies Lehmann, as Professor of Theatre Studies at Goethe University, would publish his ground-breaking study *Postdramatic Theatre* ([1999] 2006); and even closer to Giessen, where the Institute for Applied Theatre Studies at Justus Liebeg University would be a proving ground for some of the most influential European companies and directors of the late twentieth- and early twenty-first centuries. These include Rimini Protokoll, She She Pop and Rene Pollesch, making the kind of discipline-shifting performance that Lehmann wrote about (indeed, Lehmann was Associate Director of the Institute in the 1980s). Rimini Protokoll, for example, became known for their 'reality trend' theatre – something of the DNA of this is inherited from Piscator, as we shall see later.

As a young man Piscator served as a radio operator in the German army during the First World War, including service in the trenches at Ypres on the Western Front. The experience was understandably traumatic and formative. It contributed to Piscator's political migration towards communism, in a context where on the one hand warfare was a grim leveller of individual circumstance while, on the other, it seemed to the young infantryman in the trenches that working men were served up for suffering by a ruling elite (see Rorrison in Piscator [1929] 1980: 1–2; and Brecht 2015: 118). After the war, Piscator became a member of the politically radical Dada Berlin, as an actor and director. In 1919 at the Tribune Theatre he created what Mel Gordon describes as 'the first living photo-montage with one of [fellow Dadaist Richard] Huelsenbeck's sketches' (1974: 121) – an early indication of a multimedia bent. Piscator was involved in a strain of Dada that was scabrously satirical and political (a little distinct, then, from the more nonsensical flavour of the Paris and Zurich manifestations). When the Berlin Dadaists variously moved on to other things, after an intense burst of activity following the end of the war, it was no surprise that Piscator should gravitate towards a political theatre intended to be of and for the people. He co-founded *Das Proletarische Theater* (the Proletarian Theatre) in 1920 in Berlin on a subscription model, with over 5,000 members, and directed work for the company over the next couple of years. Between 1924 and 1927 Piscator was a leading director at the Volksbühne Theatre, 'the traditional stage of the workers of Berlin', as Becker notes (1970: 18); and it is at this point that *In Spite of Everything!* was made.[1]

In Spite of Everything! emerged as a concentrated element of what was intended as a longer and yet more ambitious work, following the success of Piscator's *Revue Roter Rummel* (*The Red Riot Revue*) in 1924. Becker describes this as 'a scenic montage that contained all the elements of political agitation in speech, song, poster, cabaret and sports displays which were all combined in a dramatic unity' (1970: 18) – what we might now think of as an intriguing combination of Aristotelian and (*avant la lettre*) postdramatic principles. The text is lost, but a reconstruction of sorts is possible. As Rorrison describes:

> The theme was class injustice in Germany, accompanied by a prophecy of the eventual triumph of communism ... Nightclubs and champagne bars were set against workers' slums, paunchy capitalists ... against limbless veterans ... Music, songs, acrobatics, projections, statistics, instant drawings and short sketches were used to put the message across.
>
> (in Piscator [1929] 1980: 78, 79)

Speeches from political leaders and activists Vladimir Lenin, Karl Liebknecht and Rosa Luxemburg were performed, and the show ended with a communal rendition of the socialist anthem The Internationale. Piscator himself was entirely clear about the political orientation of the production:

with a political revue I hoped to achieve propagandistic effects which would be more powerful than was possible with plays, where the ponderous structure and problems tempt you to psychologize and constantly erect barriers between the stage and the auditorium. The revue offered a chance of 'direct action' in the theatre. ... Nothing was left unclear, or ambiguous and without effect, the connection with current political events was pointed out at every turn.
(Piscator [1929] 1980: 81–3)

Persuaded by the verve, scale and political acuity of this production, the German Communist Party (KPD: *Kommunistische Partei Deutschlands*) commissioned Piscator and fellow-playwright Felix Gasbarra to make a large-scale piece of theatre for the opening of the KPD's Tenth Party Congress, scheduled to be held at the Grosses Schauspielhaus (Great Theatre) in Berlin from 12 to 17 July 1925. Piscator and Gasbarra initially wanted to present 'the revolutionary highlights of the history of mankind from the Spartacus rebellion to the Russian Revolution' (in Favorini 1995: xviii). Piscator himself described this as 'a summary in instructive scenes of the whole development of historical materialism', featuring 2,000 participants ([1929] 1980: 91). When this delicious-sounding smorgasbord of revolutions proved too extensive, Piscator settled on an 'Historical revue of the years 1914 to 1919 in twenty-four scenes with intermittent films' (as the subtitle of *In Spite of Everything!* had it). This was in effect a retelling of the history of events pertaining to the KPD over the previous decade, stitching together witness accounts, news reports and edited bulletins to relay a narrative that had Karl Liebknecht as its central protagonist. As Favorini explains, 'Presented in a review format and accompanied by music, political cartoons, moving pictures borrowed from government archives, and photographic projections, *In Spite of Everything!* created an alternative to the capitalist newspaper accounts of the same events' (1995: xviii–xix).

A century later, people might reverberate on X (the platform formerly known as Twitter) or Instagram their dissent from the postures of political parties and mainstream coverage of key events. In the 1920s, newspapers, pamphlets and sometimes books performed this function of dissensual reverberation – as well as the theatre, as long as you could find a venue that would stage your work. With the Grosses Schauspielhaus in Berlin already in the bag, performances of *In Spite of Everything!* were presented on 12 and 14 July 1925. Favorini expands upon the social and cultural influences that provide a backdrop to this work:

> The rise of the modern newspaper; the availability of archives to historians and the raising of standards for the justification of historical description; the wide acceptance of the ideas of Comte, Marx, Darwin and Spencer, who examined individual behavior in a context bound by social, economic, and physical laws; the embrace of the nineteenth-century scientific model of truth as fact supported by empirical evidence – all these exerted increasing pressure on the theatre to represent reality concretely, precisely, and directly.
>
> (1995: xviii)

This helpfully points to a cultural substrate for documentary theatre – a meld of materialist and empirical scientific and political thought, technologies of mass communication that facilitated better and more immediate news coverage, and a socio-political urgency to get at the truth of things. Piscator's production was at once sweeping and selective, dealing with instances and events with grand summation and close attention to detail. Before we look more closely at some of its component parts, let's check the historical matters with which the play deals, amid a period of churning instability in German politics during and shortly after the First World War.

A brief historical account[2]

Three key figures will concern us: Karl Liebknecht, Rosa Luxemburg and Friedrich Ebert, and their activities within and beyond the SDP (*Sozialdemokratische Partei Deutschlands*), the party of the left that at the time had the largest representation of any political party in the German parliament. On 4 August 1914, SDP members voted in the Reichstag to support war loans that would help fund the German war effort. The decision was bitterly contested, with opponents arguing that at a stroke the SDP had endorsed the imperialist venture of the war, renounced the party's traditions of pacifism and internationalism, and abandoned its alignment with the working class (see Mülhausen 2015).

Rosa Luxemburg, a pamphleteer and political activist, co-founded the International Group following a meeting at her Berlin apartment in 1914, directly in reaction to the SDP's vote to support war loans. The group quickly morphed into the Spartacus League in the same year, founded by Luxemburg along with Karl Liebknecht and Clara Zetkin (and renamed as the Spartacus Group in 1917) – so-called in honour of Spartacus, an enslaved gladiator and one of the leaders of the Third Servile War, a sustained revolt against the Roman Republic from 73 to 71 BCE. Activism in and through the Spartacists provided Liebknecht with a means of prosecuting an anti-war agenda while, initially, continuing as an SDP deputy (tactically useful since he had been the only SPD deputy to vote against the War Loan). Liebknecht was imprisoned for high treason in 1916 after giving an anti-war speech at a Spartacist demonstration; and expelled from the party. Luxemburg was also imprisoned for treason in 1916 under a preventative detention measure, and only released in 1918. She revived *Die Rote Fahne* (*The Red Flag*) as a communist newspaper in that year, with Liebknecht as co-editor, and wrote its editorials.

Division and dissent within the left rumbled on during the war. In 1917 the USPD (Independent Socialists) was constituted as a separate party for SDP defectors, formalizing the split between these different positions, and the Spartcus Group joined the USPD. On 9 November 1918, with the end of war now imminent and the military no longer responding to orders, the abdication of Kaiser Wilhelm II, the German Emperor, was announced. This followed difficult discussions between the Kaiser and his supporters – to whom it had become clear that abdication was the only path by which the allies would agree a peace treaty. Moreover, they saw that a peace treaty would potentially enable a semblance of order amid increasingly turbulent unrest, along with continuation of a form of monarchy in Germany (see Snyder 1966: 21). An armistice agreement between Germany and the allied countries was signed on 11 November 1918. Wilhelm was not enamoured of the decision concerning his abdication, and only formally abdicated on 28 November, by which time he was safely ensconced in the Netherlands. Prince Maximilien of Baden, Chancellor of the Reichstag (who had himself only been in the role for a month), asked Friedrich Ebert to take over from him as Chancellor. Ebert had become the chairman of the SDP in 1913, and was the leader whose pro-war loans position had in effect split the SDP.

On the same day, in response to fast-escalating protests and word that Liebknecht was about to declare a socialist republic, Philipp Scheidemann, Ebert's second-in-command, proclaimed a Social Democratic Republic from the balcony of the Reichstag – against the wishes of Ebert. Liebknecht, only released from prison in October and standing outside the Kaiser's palace, duly announced a soviet republic. Ebert transacted with the military to agree a damping down of social unrest in return for his support of the military's continued involvement in German political decision-making. At the end of December, USPD members left the provisional government. The Spartacists left the USPD and formed the KPD (the German Communist Party) – which held its founding congress over the new year period, 30 December 1918 to 1 January 1919. Piscator's production of *In Spite of Everything!* at the Party Congress in 1925, then, was for a political party that would have still felt new and in the process of affirming its identity amid marked political turbulence. And the events with which the play dealt were searingly raw and recent.

If we need a touchpoint for the developments that the play addresses, bear in mind that the Russian Revolution had taken place less than two years previously. On 6 November 1917 sailors on the *Aurora* had mutinied and helped the Red Guard take over the city of Petrograd. Strikes and protests in Germany coalesced alongside mutinies of soldiers and sailors (initially in Kiel on the North Sea coast), and this provided a template for what appeared at the time to be a successful large-scale popular uprising across the German federation. Councils of workers and military personnel took over ports in the North Sea and Baltic.[3] Fuelled by exhaustion with the war effort and disagreement with modes of imperial leadership, civic and popular uprisings supplanted the rule of imperial leaders. On 7 November Kurt Eisner, leader of the Independent Social Democratic Party, led a popular revolt in the Bavarian capital Munich. Soldiers refused to take down the rebels, and King Ludwig III left the city which was thereby the capital of a newly proclaimed republic. As Louis Snyder remarks, 'The end of the Wittelsbach dynasty in Bavaria had the effect of a green light all over Germany. Princes in other states followed suit and gave up their thrones' (1966: 20).

Social and political turmoil was widespread, contested and messy. In the week from 5 January 1919 there was a series of demonstrations. Richard Cavendish summarizes the swirling counter-currents at play:

> The Berlin police chief, a radical sympathiser who had just been dismissed, supplied weapons to protesters who erected barricades in the streets and seized the offices of an anti-Spartacist socialist newspaper. Calls for a general strike brought thousands of demonstrators into the centre of the city, but the Revolution Committee, which was supposed to be leading the uprising, could not agree what to do

next. Some wanted to continue with the armed insurgency, others started discussions with Ebert. Attempts to get army regiments in Berlin to join the revolt failed.

(2009)

Ebert, as Chancellor, summoned troops, and the demonstrations were suppressed in a violent set of actions. Liebknecht and Luxemburg were arrested; and attacked while en route to prison – probably by members of the *Freikorps* (a right-wing militia formed of volunteers). As Snyder reports, 'Liebknecht was killed "while seeking to escape," and Luxemburg was beaten so badly that she died a few hours later' (1966: 32). This was an awful pivotal moment, and the murders of Liebknecht and Luxemburg, tacitly approved by the SPD, confirmed a fissure in the Left that would arguably enable the rise of Hitler and the National Socialist Party (see, for instance, Arjomand 2018: 8).

These appear to be the facts. They involve the actions of individuals and groups; decisions, instructions and outcomes, transacted in highly personal and individual situations, and at epic scale involving many people and vast national and international attention. It is extremely difficult (and perhaps not possible) to piece together an exact trail of causes and effects (like a line of dominos, perhaps) since so much of this history is really a texture of co-dependent elements. A better analogy than the dominos, then, is provided by a weather system, in which a variety of elements help to determine a particular incident or situation, in an ever-shifting set of interrelations. That's not particularly neat. Nor does it quite capture the more definitive process of cause and effect when a leader issues a command, or an individual shoots another, or a group of people agree that enough is enough.

Clearly the historical record is dense with this stuff of behaviour, action, reaction and consequence. And this brings us to the heart of documentary theatre. Firstly, something happens. Secondly, the effects of the happening are felt, and groups of people attempt to make sense of it and perhaps make adjustments (to agreed perspectives, behaviours and even to policy) accordingly. Thirdly, the theatre-maker attempts to re-present what happened, and this very presentation contributes to the circulation of understandings and effects. In doing so, a number of new decisions are required. What *did* happen? How do we know this, and how do we show it? What do we turn to, that conveys the facts of the matter? What do we make of these facts? And what do we want others to make of them? How is our own personal view significant here? And how does this help shape what we show?

We shall come later to questions of the investment – indeed even involvement – of the teller in what's told. We will also come to instances of documentary theatre that make the density and difficulty of the 'record' precisely a subject of the presentation. But in our first case study, we are concerned straightforwardly with an attempt to convey the historical record – which as the potted summary, above, indicates, is by no means straightforward. How did Piscator proceed?

In Spite of Everything! – the play[4]

The text of *In Spite of Everything!* is not full and complete, but rather a list of scenes with stage directions (Piscator and Gasbarra 1995; this includes useful editorial notes by Kolb and Favorini). Nonetheless, the narrative line of the play is clear, and we can piece together its theatrical and tactical approach. *In Spite of Everything!* starts in Potsdam Square, a busy traffic intersection for buses, trams and cars, surrounded with cafes and restaurants, a place of public congregation. 'A newspaper carrier distributes extra-editions bearing the news: Assassination of the Austrian crown prince in Sarajewo. The public is made up of a mix of Social Democrats and right-wing enthusiasts who discuss the possibilities of an approaching war' (Piscator and Gasbarra 1995: 1).

From the outset, then, we are under no illusions. The play deals with the most seismic public events (referencing here the shooting of Franz Ferdinand that led to the First World War), transacts them partly through their mediation in the news outlets of the time, and expands on them by way of a staged public discourse featuring the voices of people who don't agree with each other. This might appear to be documentary as dialectical, exploring different opinions – but a guiding narrative presumption becomes clear as the scenes unfold.

The play runs chronologically. Scenes are date-stamped and set in a mix of public, civic and industrial settings – for example, Scene 3, at the Imperial Palace in Berlin, 1 August 1914, 'Wilhelm II declares war on Russia and speaks from the balcony of the palace to the people.' We don't have the text of what the various persons (a better term, here, than 'characters') said to each other within this staging, but the discourse of the play swirls around what was heard to be said in the public sphere – what was said in public, on the record, in civic proceedings and addresses to the people. There is, too, a more tightly focused kind of public speaking, one that requires invention on the part of the writers. The scenes either side of the one set at the Imperial Palace involve meetings of the Social Democratic Reichstag Faction, on 25 July and 3 August 2014 respectively. They feature party leaders, including Ebert, Landsberg and Liebknecht. In Scene 2 Liebknecht 'speaks decisively against an eventual war' (2). The dialectical mode, we assume, is played out in these party scenes too, presenting the different positions that will be dramatized in the play as a stark separation between the assertively anti-militarist Liebknecht on the one hand, and Ebert on the other, who took a managerialist and conciliatory position with respect to Germany's prosecution of the war.

Utterance, then, is textured in different ways but always focused on political matters, arguments and decisions. There is also a variety of settings presented, again insofar as they matter to depicting the narrative of events. Scene 6, set in a Berlin grenade factory, features workers demanding a strike, a call that falters when the factory's management threatens that it will rescind the exemption from active service that the factory workers enjoy. Scene 11 takes place in Treptower Park on 30 January 1918, during the Munition Workers' strike, in which 'Ebert speaks to the striking munitions workers, but the workers hiss and boo, shouting him down' (Piscator and Gasbarra 1995: 3). According to the accompanying editorial note, the strike was 'the largest political mass strike during World War I' (4).

In Spite of Everything! is celebrated for its inclusion of film within the live theatre presentation. Scene 4 ends with 'Newsreel: Mobilization, advance, the killing begins' (2).

Scene 9 ends with '*Newsreel: the Killing Goes On – authentic footage of battles from the World War*' (3, original emphasis). Newspaper reports are revealed. Scene 12: 'Potsdam Square. Extra editions are distributed [by newspaper carriers] among the groups discussing the eventuality of a revolution' (4). We will consider this multimedia aspect more closely, below.

Woven throughout is what we might call the Liebknecht narrative – tracing Liebknecht's arguments and interventions, through to his eventual assassination. Given the brevity of the textual fragments, and the distillation that the play entails, I have listed these here in sequence (Piscator and Gasbarra 1995: 2–7):

Scene 2, 25 July 2014: Liebknecht speaks against war.

Scene 5, 2 December 1914: Liebknecht votes against war credits.

Scene 7, 1 May 1916: after a jump in time, Liebknecht speaks in Potsdam Square at a First of May parade, 'and is arrested by two patrolmen'.

Scene 9, 23 August 1916: Liebknecht goes on trial before the War Tribunal. In his address, he says that the people should be allowed to decide his case.

Scene 13, 9 November 1918: this scene juxtaposes council discussions in the palace of the Imperial Chancellor and a street demonstration outside the place, in which Liebknecht – recently released from prison – declares a socialist republic backed by workers and striking soldiers.

Scene 14, Imperial chancellery, Landsberg's workroom, 5 December 1918: 'Landsberg briefs Petty Officer Krebs' that there will be a Spartacus demonstration on Chaussee Street, and that a shot will be fired from the crowd, which will be Krebs's signal to 'Use machine guns and fire upon the crowd' (5). The next scene presents this scenario.

Scene 16, In the office of the editor of *The Red Flag*: Liebknecht, Luxemburg and Radek decide what to do next.

Scene 19, 11 January 1919, depicts Liebknecht and Luxemburg in a session of the 'Revolution Committee', where Liebknecht protests against the committee's decision to negotiate with the government.

Scene 21. 'THE LAST EVENING – 15 JANUARY': Luxemburg and Liebknecht are arrested.

Scene 22, on the same evening, the reception hall of the Eden Hotel. The action depicts the briefing of the officer holding Liebknecht and Luxemburg, to the effect that they should be ushered out of the car by the lake of the zoological garden, and then shot as though they had attempted escape while the vehicle had broken down.

Scene 23, Zoological Garden. 'The car stops on the edge of the lake. Liebknecht takes two steps and is shot down.'

In the next scene, which concludes the play, 'Red Front revolutionaries march onto the stage and take position with approximately 50 men and eight flags.' The revolution, in this rendition, lives on.

The storytelling is sharply focused; and constructed to present logical connections between political initiatives and outcomes for individuals and groups. It moves with bravura speed across 'behind-the-scenes' depictions of meetings of interest groups, caucuses and political parties, to gatherings and transactions in public spaces, to the covert assassination – depicted as an explicitly political act on the part of the government.

The 'document' in documentary theatre is foregrounded, in terms of the referential texture of known events and actions, underpinned by the authorizing paraphernalia of newsreels and newspapers. The line of travel, nonetheless, is not only that of a linear narrative over the timeframe of the play (replete with mechanisms of suspense and deliverance), but also towards a gathering affirmation of the KPD's place in this history and the revolutionary position it upheld. The documentary project, here, is coolly assembled to create the heat of an affective desire for action.

Multimedia, multimodal, political, pedagogic

Piscator describes the scenography of his production as 'the abandonment of the decorative set, replaced here by the "predominant principle ... of a purely practical acting structure to support, clarify and express the action"' ([1929] 1980: 94). This structure comprised a raked platform on one side and a set of levels on the other, with 'various terraces, niches and corridors' revealed depending on the positioning of the revolve (a circular floor that could be rotated to reveal different set-ups and scenic arrangements). As Piscator said, 'In this way the overall structure of the scenes was unified and the play could flow uninterrupted, like a single current sweeping everything along with it' (94). Dramaturgically, then, the techniques of staging facilitate a view of historical process as a linear set of cause-and-effect interrelations, that together structure political action and lived experience. Piscator's 'practical' set enabled scenic transitions that expressed something of the march of history, while it also facilitated the inclusion of screens for the projection of the film segments, offering an accompanying historical fix.

FIGURE 1 *Programme sheet,* Trotz alledem! (In Spite of Everything!), *by Felix Gasbarra and Erwin Piscator, directed by Erwin Piscator, Berlin, Grosses Schauspielhaus, 12 July 1925. Image © Akademie der Künste [AdK], Berlin.*

Piscator describes the specific film material used in his production, drawn from the Reich archives and made available by a contact:

> These shots brutally demonstrated the horror of war: flame thrower attacks, piles of mutilated bodies, burning cities; war films had not yet come into "fashion," so these pictures were bound to have a more striking impact on the masses of the proletariat than a hundred lectures. I spread the film out through the whole play, and where that was not enough I projected stills.
>
> ([1929] 1980: 94)

Piscator reflects later in his chapter on the 'drastic effect' (he uses the adjective in a positive sense) of the use of film clips. 'The momentary surprise when we changed from live scenes to film was very effective. But the dramatic tension that live scene and film clip derived from one another was even stronger. They interacted and built up each other's power' (97).

You can sense the director's pride and excitement. In other respects, Piscator is engagingly modest and phlegmatic in his account of the combination of different art forms in the production. He mentions that the use of film clips was developed from earlier work on the production *Flags* at the Volksbühne in 1923 and before that his work in Königsberg. 'All I did was to extend and refine the means; the aim stayed the same' (93). You might assume that Piscator was familiar with the montage-based editing of Russian film-makers including Sergei Eisenstein, whose film *Battleship Potemkin* was released in the same year that *In Spite of Everything!* was staged, while Eisenstein's film *Strike* had been released the previous year (1924). Piscator's use of film in theatre was tactically similar to the aesthetic of cinematic montage, in its juxtaposition of different elements in order for the spectator to create logical connections. Piscator states, however, that he was unaware of experiments with film on the Soviet stage at the time, noting that any similarities 'would merely prove that this was no superficial game with technical effects, but a new, emergent form of theater based on the philosophy of historical materialism which we shared' (93). Film, he says, provided a means by which facts could be shared, and their effects on different classes and individuals made clear. 'But it was no more than a means, and could be replaced tomorrow by some better means' (94).

For Brecht (likewise a canny navigator of means and ends), Piscator's use of film and film projections was one of his 'far-reaching innovations', and Brecht describes the film as 'a new, gigantic actor that helped to narrate events' (2015: 120). You can see both the dramaturgical and scenographic implications. The inclusion of film content is deliberately dovetailed with live action in a way that creates meaning in the moment of viewing; whilst also requiring particular scenic and infrastructural solutions to allow for film projection at sufficient scale on a stage suited to live drama.

In 1926 Piscator commissioned the architect Walter Gropius (founder of the Bauhaus in Weimar) to design the 'Piscator Theatre', and it's worth dwelling briefly on the principles of this commission, since it indicates the deliberate conception of a kind of theatre intended to be theatrical in terms of the physical co-presence of actors and audience, whilst geared around plural mediation. Gropius's account tells us something about the ambition of the project and its aspiration to enable a cross-media kind of production:

> I produced a plan which included all three classic stage forms [apron, proscenium and arena stages] ... all in one theatre ... Film projectors were located all round the sides of the theatre, some pointing at the roof, so that scenery could be created behind and above the spectators as well, thus giving them the illusion of being totally involved in the drama ... Black Friday [the bank crash of 1929] put an end to our hopes.
> (Gropius 1970: 35. See also Piscator [1929] 1980: 180–3, which includes Gropius's account)

A shame, then, that this multimedia theatre venue was never realized – prefiguring as it does the kind of technical infrastructure used for multimedia performance and events many decades later; and offering itself as an early intimation of immersive cross-media production. On the one hand, then, Piscator's conception of a theatre that was saturated in reality led to forward-looking aspirations concerning architectural and infrastructural spaces for performance. But it also based itself on an historical inheritance of technical aptitude and capacity in the wider German theatre scene. In his study of Piscator's work, John Willett reflects on the legacy of a court theatre infrastructure in the small kingdoms and principalities that made up the constellation of Germany at the time as a nation state:

> No theatre in Europe could compete with the German in the resourcefulness of its technicians (who were the first to develop electric stage lighting, the revolving stage and other modern devices), in the security offered to its actors or in the opportunities open to its playwrights. It was quite simply more professional than any other.
> (Willett [1978] 1986: 42)

Credit, then, to Piscator for the ambition in his staging – while noting that he was able to draw on a settled and advanced professional theatre structure that underpinned the cross-media production processes that he brought together. As ever, we should consider what's produced alongside the infrastructures on which it draws.

If this is documentary theatre as a multimedia production number, it is also multimodal. As communications theorists suggest, a medium of communication can involve distinct modalities (that is, different ways of communicating, with different characteristics). Think of the difference, for example, between a symbol on a road sign, which operates through rapid understanding of a commonly agreed signification; and an informational leaflet, which presumes a more extended time of individual attention precisely to gain understanding. Each of the modalities operates by way of various modes.

Communicative modes can include written texts, visual images, diagrams, typography, facial gestures and nods of the head (see, for example, Bateman et al. 2017: 16; Djonov and Zhao 2014: 1; Fernandes 2016: 1). In the example above, both the road sign and leaflet might say the same thing about an environment in which deer may run across the road – one does so through a symbol that conveys a warning, the other through text and images in a factual register. A key principle is the transactional nature of modes: their work as communicative elements within a process of signification. As Gunter Kress suggests, '*Mode* is a socially shaped and culturally given resource for making meaning' ([2009] 2014: 60, original emphasis; see also Jewitt [2009] 2014: 22).

Piscator's *In Spite of Everything!* is multimodal in its combination of found materials, citations from news reports, quotations from pamphlets, film sequences and theatrical staging. The fact of combination (and indeed the combination of facts) is important both in generating a gathered view of the events depicted and in demanding a sense-making process on the part of the spectator. Bateman et al. observe that 'Modes presented together then need to be interpreted with respect to one another and so cannot be considered independently' (2017: 17) This is not a million miles from the kind of 'active' spectatorship that Brecht theorized in his account of 'epic' theatre and the request that it makes of the spectator to piece together the components of what they see, in the moment that they are seeing it.

In Brecht's account, it was the business of drama to show how events unfolded through a meeting of socio-political context and individual choices and actions (see, for instance, 'Short Description of a New Technique of Acting That Produces a Verfremdung Effect', in Brecht [2015: 184–96]). In this Brechtian sense, 'epic' theatre rejects the Aristotelian premise that a drama should be arranged to produce classical consistencies of unbroken time and space, or 'bourgeois' consistencies of character. Instead, it should present a narrative that can deal with interrelated actions and consequences. There were clear overlaps between the thinking of both Brecht and Piscator, particularly to do with an emphasis on human action in a materialist context – that's to say, choices that are determined at least as much by political and social forces as by individual feelings; and a preference for a form of theatre that was episodic and (to differing degrees) multimodal. This required the kind of 'stitching' by director (and indeed the spectator) that produced significance out of scenic storytelling. Piscator gives the following example: 'when the Social Democratic vote on War Loans (live) was followed by a film showing the first dead, it not only made the political nature of the procedure clear, but also produced a shattering human effect, became art, in fact' ([1929] 1980: 97).

Brecht would lay claim to the conception of 'epic theatre' as both an approach and a dramaturgical strategy although, as Willett observes, 'As early as 1926 Brecht was seeing Piscator as a contributor to that "great epic and documentary theatre" which was on the way' (Willett [1978] 1986: 186.) Piscator certainly provides an early model for Brecht's 'epic' theatre in this combination of elements that nonetheless remain distinct rather than fused. In the *Messingkauf Dialogues* Brecht observes that:

> For some time Piscator's followers argued with the Augsburger's about which of the two had invented the epic style of representation [the 'Augsburger' is Brecht himself]. In fact they were both using it at the same time in different cities – in Piscator's case, more in relation to the stage (in the use of captions, choruses, films etc.), in the Augsburger's case more in relation to acting style. Both of them were in fact just acknowledging the medium of film in their theatre.
> (2014: 69–70)

And while Brecht is somewhat self-aggrandizing ('It is the Augsburger who must be credited with formulating the actual theory of non-Aristotelian theatre') he acknowledges the overlapping but distinctive work of his peer. Piscator, he says, worked 'in a completely independent and original way.

Above all, the theatre's conversion to politics was Piscator's achievement, and without this conversion the Augsburger's theatre would scarcely be conceivable' (in Brecht 2014: 121).

We can understand this work in a wider context of German cultural production, to do with a conception (well established by the twentieth century) of theatre as an arena for social and political debate. This ran alongside a newer project, whereby theatre practice was in service not only of entertainment but also of education and experimentation, providing for new understandings in both pedagogy and production. By the time of *In Spite of Everything!*, workers' educational societies, performances at political meetings and amateur theatre groups all meshed to form a substantial texture of people's theatre, protesting, explaining, arguing. Lutz Becker notes that 'From the foundation of an organized labour movement in the middle of the nineteenth century, there has been a proletarian theatre in Germany; a theatre fighting for the liberation of the working class' (Becker 1970: 13). Piscator drew on this tradition and, as we have already seen, founded the Proletarian Theatre in Berlin in 1920. *In Spite of Everything!* sits firmly within this deliberately class-based dramatic inheritance. We have, then, a quasi-professionalized theatre circuit, and a demotic performance scene that was used to commenting, arguing and critiquing in and through theatre. To this we can add the development of studio-based experimentation and small-scale pedagogic performance, fusing enquiries into theatre form with the socio-political project of explaining social and political circumstances and determinants.

This is the case across Europe in the period before and after the First World War (as exemplified by Antoine's Théâtre Libre in Paris; the British Drama League, founded by Geoffrey Whitworth; and the Moscow Art Theatre Studio, which Meyerhold ran for a time). The entry for 1929 in Hugh Rorrison's 'Chronological Table of Political and Theatrical Events' gives something of the flavour of such developments in Germany: '*The Piscator-Bühne Studio* [established in 1927] *is followed by the Volksbühne Studio, the Novemberstudio (organized by*

A. Granach) and the Studio Dresdner Schauspieler ... Brecht directs his first Lehrstück at Baden-Baden' (in Piscator [1929] 1980: 362, original emphasis; the chronology is 345–367). As Rorrison notes, 'The Piscator-Bühne Studio was set up ... to provide a framework within which the techniques of political theater could be explored and developed. It offered theory courses and practical exercises' (in Piscator [1929] 1980: 285). There isn't space here to unpack the work that was undertaken in these studios, but their mention hints at the prevailing interest in artistic experimentation along with pedagogy, and the connection of training for theatre craft with social analysis – a project that Piscator would pursue again in the United States in the 1940s.[5]

Documentary and storytelling

I've suggested above that Piscator's production of *In Spite of Everything!* sought to depict the historical record. It does so by turning to newsreel footage and newspaper accounts, and to the substance of dramatic theatre: scenes between individuals (whom we understand to be historical figures). These are rather 'behind the scenes' evocations of the stories in the news. In this sense, 'news' is re-rendered both as affirming actuality and expanded (imagined) re-enactment. And this brings us to another feature of *In Spite of Everything!* It trades in storytelling. It selects and presents its scenarios in order to tell interweaving stories: one of the dissolution of Germany's Left amid a dilemma concerning compliance or resistance; one that more specifically addresses the gathering agenda of the KPD, so pertinent to Piscator's audience during the Tenth Party Congress; and one concerning the deaths of Luxemburg and Liebknecht, here stitched into the Liebknecht narrative.

I don't mean to go down the rabbit-hole here of narrative theory and the history of epistemology, but I do want to suggest that – however sharp its focus on facticity – documentary theatre and performance are often profoundly concerned with storytelling. This isn't a particularly earth-shattering observation, but it does cue us to be mindful of tropes and techniques of narration; to do with legibility, sequence, action and consequence, and outcomes for individuals and groups. Maria Ley-Piscator (Piscator's wife from 1937 until his death) dates Piscator's stylistic investment in narrative to his production of *Flags* by Alphonse Pacquet at the Volksbühne in 1924 where, she suggests, 'Piscator found his style, a theatre between narration and drama' (Ley-Piscator 1967: 75).

This returns us to the purpose of *In Spite of Everything!*, and its structuring of documentary facticity along a dramatic arc. Piscator was keenly aware of wanting to create a direct engagement with working-class audiences through a different kind of dramatic presentation than that of a more literary form of drama. Different but not entirely foreign in its dramatic trajectory – indeed, more immediate precisely *because of* its combination of subject matter and mode of presentation. As Piscator said:

> For the first time we were confronted with the absolute reality we knew from experience. And it had exactly the same moments of tension and dramatic climaxes as literary drama, and the same strong emotional impact. Provided, of course, that it was a political reality ("political" in the original sense: "being of general concern").
>
> (1980: 96)

For all that, the production of *In Spite of Everything!* had only two performances. For the first, as Piscator describes it, 'Every seat was taken, steps, aisles, entrances were full to bursting' ([1929] 1980: 96). The anticipation of the audience apparently shifted into an extraordinarily close engagement – closer perhaps, as Piscator moots, given that the facts presented were still raw. 'The people who filled the house had for the most part been actively involved in the period, and what we were showing them was in a true sense their own fate, their own tragedy being acted out before their eyes. Theater had become reality' (96).

Towards the end of his chapter on the production in *The Political Theatre*, Piscator understandably includes some cuttings from press reviews and subsequent writings. One describes how, in the drama, Liebknecht 'is arrested, and as the mob lets him be taken away without protest, cries of anguish and self-accusation are heard in the audience' (from 'How It Began', *Frankfurter Zeitung*, 1 April 1929; cited in Piscator [(1929) 1980: 97]). This is, perhaps, a fitting testimony to work that sought to educate, entertain and provoke to action.

In another cutting, Jacob Altmeier, writing in the *Frankfurter Zeitung*, described the distinction between the 'bourgeois' theatre that Piscator sought to supplant and the work that he had presented to his audience:

> Jessner might work wonders with *The Death of Wallenstein* … and Reinhardt might spread heaven at our feet with *Twelfth Night* … But after a revue like this you felt as if you had had a bath. You had new strength. You could swim and row in the streets. Traffic and lights, the roar and the machines all made sense.
> (cited in Piscator [1929] 1980: 97–8)

Piscator ends his chapter with the bitter reflection that, although the second performance was full and 'hundreds could not get in', he was unable to have the show extended for any further nights since 'the authorities were afraid to take the risk' – meaning that in his view 'even this stage in the development of the political theater achieved no real outward progress' ([1929] 1980: 98). This opens up the question as to that other relation between art and reality: not the one that takes real events and turns them into an artwork, but the one where the artwork itself produces change in the socio-cultural scene in which it operates. We will ponder this later. For now, however, we pause to savour Altmeier's reflection: 'Traffic and lights, the roar and the machines all made sense.' The contemporary world, the fabric within which we live, *makes better sense, and feels different* because of watching the work. This change-function, articulated in such definitive form by Brecht a few years after *In Spite of Everything!*, provides one cornerstone of our engagement with documentary theatre and performance. Suitably arranged, it brings us up to date and aligns us with our historical moment, and in consequence we feel differently charged.

From Europe to the United States

Having established himself as a leading producer, artistic director and director of expressly political theatre, Piscator founded the Piscator-Bühne at Berlin's Theater am Nollendorfplatz in 1927, moving to the Wallner Theatre in Berlin in 1930. He left Germany when the Nazis came to power, travelling to the USSR in 1931, where he seems to have worked mainly on film projects. In 1936 he took a trip to Paris, and then took the advice issued in Bernhard Reich's two-word telegram – *Nicht Abreisen* ('Don't Return') – not to return to the USSR, which was sliding into the Stalinist purges (see Malina 2012: 10). He left Paris in 1939 for the United States, which became his home for the next thirteen years.

Cross-pollination between the United States and the USSR in terms of radical and experimental art practice had already become a phenomenon, even if initially this was more in spirit than through more formal exchanges. Maria Ley-Piscator discusses how Piscator and his colleagues in Germany in the 1920s had invented an 'America' of their desire, drawn as they were towards what might be thought an American tempo, landscape and exoticism:

> None of them had seen America ... [but] They admired what seemed real to them: the objective existence of the

land of plenty, its material genius, with its prosperity, its slogans, and the great god – the machine. It is impossible to understand the complexity of Epic Theatre without taking into account this capture of the imagination by America, while, at the same time, the period was idealistically entangled with the new Russia.

(Ley-Piscator 1967: 26)

To provide a brief snapshot of some of the cross-currents of this period, following Favorini (1995: xii) we can connect Piscator's travels from Germany to the USSR to the United States with those of two eminent American theatre artists, Hallie Flanagan and Joseph Losey. Flanagan visited Germany and Russia as a Guggenheim Fellow in 1926 and 1927, returning to Russia in 1931, the year of Piscator's arrival in the country. She became National Director of the Federal Theatre Project – established as an arm of President Roosevelt's Works Progress Administration programme under the New Deal, which provided jobs on public works programmes to unemployed Americans. The FTP under Flanagan oversaw the inception of the 'Living Newspaper Unit', formalizing – as a major socio-artistic project – the kind of reality-based, current-affairs-oriented theatre that Piscator had presented the previous decade.

Joseph Losey – who went on to direct films including *M* (1951), *The Servant* (1963) and *The Go-Between* (1971) – collaborated with Brecht and Eisler, spent the larger part of 1935 in Russia and translated Piscator's *Political Theatre* during this period. In 1936, freshly returned to the United States from Russia, he directed the celebrated Federal Theatre project *Triple-A Plowed Under*, the first publicly presented Living Newspaper production (the inaugural project, *Ethiopia*, wasn't staged). The play critiqued the Agricultural Adjustment Act (the 'triple-A' of the title), passed in 1933, which legislated for a federal system of compulsory purchases and subsidies designed to stabilize economic outcomes and address over-production in the US farming industry. Favorini notes that

'Losey was largely responsible for introducing Piscator's stage vocabulary into the Living Newspapers, not only the epic scene progression but also his technical innovations: multilevel sets, projections, loudspeakers, and an ironic juxtaposition of live stage image with cool and objective projected image' (1995: xxii).[6]

By the time Piscator arrived in the United States in 1939, then, he connected with an experimental theatre culture that was influenced by his previous work or at least resonated and was politically aligned with it. For his part, he was already attuned to – indeed was a sophisticated transactor of – the artistic currents running through reality-inflected performance East and West. No wonder then that by the end of 1939, as Willett describes, 'he was offered the job of running a Dramatic Workshop at the New School of Social Research, a New York adult education college staffed largely by eminent European exiles' (Willett 1970: 7). With its pedagogic focus and its European expat staffing, the New School was known as 'The University in Exile' (Malina 2012: 11). Its work involved the delivery of various classes along with productions – and as we have seen, Piscator's earlier experience had provided something of a template. Here he was, then – after the Dadaist, modernist, actuality-driven theatre of the 1920s and 1930s – working in New York at a pivotal, inceptual moment of North American dramatic realism. Marlon Brando, Tony Curtis, Rod Steiger, Sylvia Miles, Walter Matthau, Eli Wallach, Shelley Winters, Tennessee Williams and Judith Malina studied at the Dramatic Workshop. Their teachers included Herbert Berghof, Stella Adler and Lee Strasberg – each subsequently opened their own school, and their legacy continues in actor training to this day. Ley-Piscator describes some overarching principles of the venture, including a key duality 'described later in a phrase that became popular: *A school that is a theatre*' (Ley-Piscator 1967: 103, original emphasis). She recounts some questions from students:

> How is great theatre put together? ... What is the basis of it all? Art or life?

"Not art," said Piscator. "Life. From its very beginning here at the Workshop, let it be life. The Here and the Now. Art is man's ambition to create beyond reality. What is needed now is reality." (1967: 105. Ley-Piscator's chapter 'Dramatic Workshop' [99–122] gives a good account of establishing the workshop, along with its principles and people.)

Actors like Brando and Steiger moved this principle into canonical character-based performances in Hollywood cinema. Judith Malina took it into her work with Julian Beck and the Living Theatre, foregrounding experimentation, political engagement and artistic radicalism. Malina was a student at Piscator's Dramatic Workshop from February 1945 to January 1947. Much of her book on Piscator is drawn from notes that she made from classes that took place between 5 February and 27 April 1945 (see Malina 2012: 36–120). She reminisces that in his lessons, Piscator:

> wanted absolute attention, absolute concentration, but above all he asked the performer to change her focus. He called this Objective Acting, in which the object of the actor's focus is the spectator ... What mattered to Piscator was intensity without emotion in the communication. If this was authentic, it would induce the actor to find the means to make the communication complete.
> (Malina 2012: 2, 150)

This perspective contributed to what Malina describes as 'result direction', which is action-oriented rather than character-based (see Malina 2012: 21–2). 'Result direction' is a useful tag for this approach, and we see the principle at work across all stages of Piscator's directorial career.

A different kind of reality-check marked Piscator's time with the Dramatic Workshop. As with his directorship of venues and companies in Germany before the Second World War, this was a story of accumulating expenditures – for example, renting theatres that the organization could barely afford – and the Dramatic Workshop closed in 1951.

West Germany and *The Investigation*

In 1951 Piscator returned to Germany, now divided into zones following the Potsdam Agreement in 1945. He initially encountered some difficulty in establishing himself in a new post-war theatre scene, and worked as a jobbing theatre director. In 1962 he became the director of the newly established Theater der Freien Volksbühne in Berlin, a post that he held until his death in 1966 at the age of 72. As Hugh Rorrison says, 'In a sense he had come home. This time the documentary plays which had been lacking during the Weimar Republic began to appear' (in Piscator [1929] 1980: 344). These included Rolf Hochhuth's *The Deputy*, Heinar Kipphardt's *In the Matter of J. Robert Oppenheimer* (both of which Piscator directed in 1963) and Peter Weiss's *The Investigation* (presented the following year). As Piscator noted in his diary: 'I must find plays that are hard, difficult, soaked in reality – as never before. Back to the style of the "twenties"' (in Hoffmann 1970: 27).

Well, back to the 1920s, but with some differences and adjustments. This final period of Piscator's life proved something of a swansong and brings us to a next stage of documentary theatre production, which we can consider by briefly examining Piscator's production of Peter Weiss's *The Investigation*. The play addresses proceedings from the Frankfurt war trials, relating to the work of those involved in managing, servicing and policing the concentration camp at Auschwitz, and the experiences of those inmates who had survived (see Favorini 1995: xxvi–xxix for a discussion of the play and production, and its notably mixed reception). It does so through a number of dramaturgical tactics, including compression and summation of aspects of the proceedings, the re-voicing of different testimonies into a single speaker's utterance, and a distinction between the witnesses who were victims (who are unnamed) and the accused (who are identified). Given that the trials ran from 20 December 1963 to 19 August 1965, this editorial work by the playwright seems entirely justified if the business of theatre is to represent in a couple of hours processes that might take considerably longer. After all, the playwright is a cartographer of culture, and no map-maker produces a map of the world that is the same size as the world. Nonetheless, you can see immediately one reason for the controversy raised by the play, with critics protesting 'that Weiss had grossly distorted the "truth" about Auschwitz' (see Favorini 1995: xxvii). Yet what was that truth?

In 1949 Theodor Adorno had stated, in a celebrated coinage, that 'after Auschwitz, to write a poem is barbaric' (Adorno [1967] 1981: 34). In other words, the production of art is insufficient, indeed unethical, in face of the scale of desecration and suffering represented by the Holocaust. The philosopher Slavoj Žižek finesses Adorno's provocation:

> Adorno's famous saying, it seems, needs correction: it is not poetry that is impossible after Auschwitz, but rather *prose*. Realistic prose fails, where the poetic evocation of the unbearable atmosphere of a camp succeeds. That is to say, when Adorno declares poetry impossible (or, rather, barbaric) after Auschwitz, this impossibility is an enabling impossibility: poetry is always, by definition, 'about' something that cannot be addressed directly, only alluded to.
> (Žižek 2008: 4)

Poetry, then, is adequate (for this topic, at least) only if allusive rather than realist. Documentary, in all its reality-affection, might be thought even more unviable. Adorno's comment was made at the end of an essay entitled 'Cultural Criticism and Society' that critiques tendencies within cultural criticism, and indeed the work of critics. It does so by making a larger argument against a totalizing effect of cultural production in late capitalism, in which 'mass' culture entails a kind of coercive drive to an 'integrated' society that does not facilitate independent thought or perspective. As Adorno says: 'The materialistic transparency of culture has not made it more honest, only more vulgar. By relinquishing its own particularity, culture has also relinquished the salt of truth, which once consisted in its opposition to other particularities' ([1967] 1981: 34).[7]

This presents a yet sharper challenge to documentary theatre, but also potentially an avenue for the representation of that which might appear unrepresentable. Documentary theatre is hardly 'poetic' in the sense that Žižek suggests, for it is to do with facticity rather than allusion, and its registers are closer to that of 'realistic prose' in its turn to writing and utterances in the public sphere. However, this rhetorical and aesthetic structure also distinguishes it from more fictional dramatic representation (as in, for example, plays written by authors who invent the speaking of their characters, even if this is conveyed in a realist idiom). The trial-based play is indeed not poetic, but nor is it an act of artistic imagination in the sense that Adorno implies. Its very basis in actuality (the record of the trial proceedings) provides a conduit to understanding something of the institutional and individual processes by which the events of the Holocaust took place and were experienced. As Arjomand suggests, 'Piscator sought to find a new form of documentary political theatre at a moment when the inadequacies of theatrical representation were keenly felt' (Arjomand 2018: 14; Arjomand considers Žižek's essay, cited above, in this section).

Weiss himself was adamant that his process was focused on actuality, at the service of coherent representation, arguing to this end in 'Fourteen Propositions for a Documentary Theater':

> The documentary theatre shuns all invention. It makes use of authentic documentary material which it diffuses from the stage, without altering the contents, but in structuring the form ... it does not pretend to vie in authenticity

with the Nuremburg trial, with the Auschwitz trial at Frankfurt … thanks to the remoteness it enjoys, it can argue from effect to cause and thus complete the hearings from the points of view which were not presented at the original trial.
(reproduced in Favorini 1995: 139, 142; originally published in 1968)

The documentary theatre, then, is accurate and non-inventive, whilst making sense of things precisely by way of its 'remoteness', its distance (to a point, at least) in time and perhaps place from the original proceedings. As Weiss suggests, 'The documentary theatre can also introduce the public into the heart of the proceedings' (in Favorini 1995: 142). This is precisely what Piscator sought to do in his production of *The Investigation*. It reverberated with previous work in which Piscator explored judicial transaction, cross-media scenography and audience engagement. His production of *S218* (1929), for example, featured actors planted in the audience who gave quasi-professional perspectives on abortion, before Piscator opened out to a general discussion on the issue at the end of the show. In New York over twenty years later, Piscator had directed a production of *The Burning Bush* (1949) based on transcripts from a court case in 1884 in what is now northern Hungary (Arjomand 2018: 97; 101–10). Arjomand summarizes the approach as one that responded 'to the problem of representing atrocity by representing atrocity through diegesis rather than mimesis' (2018: 15) – in other words, narrating incidents through questioning and testimony rather than dramatic representation. By the end of the 1960s, then, Piscator and the playwrights with whom he was working shaped a form of documentary performance that would become standardized by the 1980s and 1990s as testimony-based, tribunal and verbatim theatre in the UK and the United States.

In the case of *The Investigation*, the trial proceedings had already become a form of public theatre even before being remediated in the Theater der Freien Volksbühne. Around 20,000 people watched the proceedings in the courthouse in Frankfurt over the two years in which they took place; and the trial was hugely significant, as part of the wider post-Holocaust process of reckoning in West Germany, in bringing charges against a range of individuals at all levels of operation for their part in the genocide (Arjomand 2018: 111). The wide geopolitical resonance of the trial was underscored in and through Piscator's conception of the production of *The Investigation* as an international event rather than a localized opening at a single venue. As Arjomand explains:

> Piscator issued a call for theaters across both East and West Germany to join in the play's premiere. It opened simultaneously in fifteen German cities (Peter Brook also held a staged reading in London) [in the event, nine of the productions were fully staged, the others were readings] ... In the weeks preceding the premiere alone, more than one thousand articles about the play appeared in East and West Germany.
>
> (2018: 111)

An excerpt from the play illustrates the dramaturgical approach. The judge is questioning a witness about the reception and sorting of prisoners on the railway platform on disembarkation from the train bringing people to the camp.

5TH WITNESS:
...
    The officer who divided us
    was very friendly
    I asked him
    where the others were going
    and he said
    They're just going to shower now
    You'll see them again in an hour
JUDGE:
    Does the witness
    know who this officer was

5TH WITNESS:
I found out later
that his name was Dr Capesius

(Weiss 1995: 49)

Asked by the judge, the witness identifies one of the defendants as Dr Capesius. The defendant ('Accused #3' in the playtext) asserts that the witness must have confused him for someone else. At this a sixth witness, a doctor, identifies Capesius as one of his patients. He recounts an exchange they had on the platform on disembarking from the train, when Capesius had assured the man that 'Everything's going to be fine here'.

JUDGE:
There is no doubt in your mind
that that man was Dr Capesius
6TH WITNESS:
No
I spoke with him
At the time it was a great pleasure for me
to see him again

(Weiss [1965] 1995: 49)

The dialogue is curated from the trial proceedings. Its layout, with minimal punctuation and each phrase on a different line, displays in the textual format the segments of utterance that comprise the questions and responses. This is not poetry in the sense alluded to above, but it does mark a journey that distances the playtext from the original court proceedings, as if the aesthetic arrangement seeks to spread the utterance on the microscope glass provided by theatrical organization.

Judith Malina describes the scenic arrangement:

> The set for The Investigation was a huge courtroom that seemed to enclose the audience ... Here was space. And behind the semi-circle of the interrogated, Piscator's stage

designer Hans-Ulrich Schmückle had suspended huge screens, on which the faces of the accused were televised, so that even as they spoke we could examine their expressions in a manner beyond what the theatre usually allows. By using the technique of the cinematic close-up, Piscator permitted the audience to share in the investigation.
(Malina 2012: 164)

In addition, 'intense musical sections by the great Italian composer, Luigi Nono, were interspersed between scenes' (Malina 2012: 163). We are back with the technological multi-component performance exemplified by *In Spite of Everything!*, but with a different kind of focus – more forensic by way of the procedure of the trial itself, more granular in its turn to actuality and presented with an invitation to scrutinize, not least through the use of live-relay close-ups projected at large scale. This arrangement made the theatre arguably more immediate to its public because more cinematic, indeed more televisual – Piscator again harnessing contemporary media forms in service of a theatre that concentrates meaning for its audience.

On experience and insufficiency

Let's briefly consider Piscator's productions in the light of the key categories of documentary theatre that I discussed in the introductory chapter to this volume. This is work that stakes a claim to document the incidents with which it deals. It does so retrospectively in the case of *In Spite of Everything!*, drawing on newspaper accounts and replaying newsreel footage. This is a 'theatre of the real' in its depiction of actual historical incidents and its turn to materials from other media that had already been circulated in the public domain. However, the documentation is presented in order to reveal the connections between events and recommend a political position accordingly. Broadly, the theatre production is an act of revelation and intervention. I've suggested that we consider documentary theatre by way of the experience that it presents and/or organizes. In *Spite of Everything!* arranges its material to inspire and indeed mobilize its audience – no surprise, given the function of the piece as part of the proceedings of the German Communist Party's Tenth Party Congress.

It dwells rather less on the experience of the protagonists with which it deals. They are presented as actors in the historical sense, individuals whose decisions and actions contribute to civic and political process. By 1965 and *The Investigation*, a slightly different negotiation of experience is afoot. The latter play necessarily dwells upon the experiences of the individuals who provide witness testimony, and the spectator is asked to adjudicate this, both for the veracity of the telling and the implications (for human interrelation, for ideas of behaviour and social justice) of the experiences that are described. This produces a differently affective kind of viewing – arguably not the 'cries of anguish' of a committed crowd that Piscator describes ([1929] 1980: 97), but a more reflective kind of engagement. Nonetheless, the perspectives that Piscator sought to organize were in service of a social and political vision, one that held as self-evident the structuring realities that the plays sought to reveal. In both pieces – and across Piscator's career – the notion of truth was relatively stable, and it was the job of the documentary theatre-maker to uncover the truth that seemed to be there; and mobilize its audience in relation to what this truth revealed.

For all that, I'd like to end this section by recognizing the insufficiency of the documentation that I've consulted. The playtext of *In Spite of Everything!*, as indicated above, exists only in partial and sketchy form. It doesn't include dialogue, but only scene outlines and stage directions. The document is already selected, mediated, edited – we can say the same of any documentary theatre text, but this set of structuring gaps is all the more marked when there is no 'playtext' to speak of. With respect to *The Investigation*, where there is very definitely a playtext (put together by a talented playwright), Adorno's drastic statement continues to haunt the proceedings. However much is uncovered, can we really, properly accommodate (in our understanding, our emotional scope) the substance of the experiences that are evoked? Any document can itself perform power, subjugation, determination, omission. And our turn to the document in documentary theatre is always already full of potential, but also fissured and depends upon a gap, for the originary document (whether it be news footage, courtroom testimony, archival record) is fundamentally distinct from the lived experience of embodied and experiential engagement. And yet, our own engagement in the moment is surely real to us, and this is where theatre makes a mark anew. It re-inscribes a figure of the real in our present engagement. The next three plays that we consider attempt just that. We move to a pair of dramas in the United States and one in the UK, part of the flowering of testimony and tribunal theatre in the 1990s for which *The Investigation* provided an early model.

3

Verbatim Theatre, Documentary Theatre and contests for civic change: 1992, 1993, 1999

We left off in the last chapter in 1965. Let's fast forward by about thirty years and turn to three celebrated productions in the 1990s that respond to major instances of civic disturbance and judicial process in the United States and UK. They operate right at the intersection between communities and their police forces, and between the experience of single individuals and forms of civic process that run from government to the law courts via the police, the media and community interrelations. To put it another way, they address what happens in the aftermath of murder and beatings, why people are moved to riot and how society either closes down proper scrutiny or finds a way to open it up. Each of these pieces advanced the theatre forms of their time. I shall outline the productions and their context, and dwell on some key issues for documentary performance – particularly as they relate to the issue of racism, an abiding socio-political fault line over centuries. As we shall see, both the events that the plays deal with and the theatre productions themselves bring racism into a lurid spotlight.

This exemplifies the kind of illumination that documentary theatre brought to various topics over this period.

Anna Deavere Smith

We start with the work of an individual concerned to present collections of individuals – the American actor, writer and director Anna Deavere Smith. The term 'writer' requires special contextualization. Born in 1950 in Baltimore, Maryland to African American parents, Smith's biography demonstrates a personal journey navigating class and colour lines, and the same is true of her writing and performing. (For a biographical overview published on the occasion of Smith's delivery of the Jefferson Lecture in 2015, see NEH 2015.) She made a name for herself through a distinctive mode of documentary performance, based on re-presenting the utterances of individuals whom she had interviewed. 'Writing' in this instance is a combination of selection of interviewees, decision concerning questions, transcription of answers and editorial arrangement. Smith selects material pertinent to the topic of the respective theatre production; and arranges it in juxtaposition with other interview material to create a constellation of perspective and response. This is, in effect, a form of expanded thematic curation, geared around individuals who variously represent larger communities and demographics, and are presented as part of a wider socio-cultural texture.

Smith's dramaturgical method holds multiple utterances in play. This is an effect of serialization – characters are presented one by one, so that they accumulate perspectives on a topic, and Deavere Smith appears not to editorialize but rather to gather and display. The work is oriented around matters of identity and affiliation across different members of a community, the ostensible purpose being to present the community in its (presumed) entirety. *Gender Bending: On the Road* (1982–83), for example, addressed men-only policies in eating clubs at Princeton University. *On the Road: Voices of Bay Area Women in Theater*, presented several women talking about the theatre industry. Works such as these helped Smith establish a template procedure as part of an ongoing project entitled 'On the Road: A Search for American Character'. The singular last word might make the initiative seem reductive, but in her theatre productions it becomes clear that Smith's quest is to unearth a plurality of characters rather than a single agglomerated American citizen; and disparate individuals are brought together in a kind of culture clash within a single thematic frame.[1]

This means that the term 'actor' also requires some finessing. Deavere Smith typically plays all the characters in bravura one-woman shows. She does not really inhabit the individuals represented in a method-based mode of performance, although she is interested in her subjects precisely as 'characters' (see Smith 1994: xviii–xxiv). Instead, she re-presents them – Smith's preferred term is 're-iterating' (Weatherston 2008: 200) – in what we might think of as a more detached style. This performance is Brechtian, perhaps, in its implication that characters can be quickly put on and taken off, so to speak; while mimicking as closely as possible the postures, gestures and vocal tendencies of the respective individual, who is further signified through specific items of costume. There is a trace of comic bravura (the changes of tack of the stand-up comic, perhaps; the knowing closeness to irony), but the project is notably earnest. Arjomand suggests that 'Like Brecht, Smith finds and distils social *Gestus*, a manner of acting that conveys the historical and social situatedness of each character. But she also presents each character with a voice that asks to be heard in all its particularity' (2018: 174–5). For Smith, 'Nobody talks alike. So I thought that one place to study identity would be in the actual speech of a given person ... individuality as it is captured in the actual physiological mechanism of making sounds' (Smith n.d.; see NEH [2015] on a preference for accessing work through language rather than method-like emotional memory and individual back-story; see Weatherston [2008: 189–90] for a reflection upon Smith's related experiments with speech patterns and a non-immersive method of acting). Smith is a refractor as much as an actor – re-voicing speech in a kaleidoscopic collation, so that the segments accumulate a pattern of (often notably divergent) individual experience that the spectator is asked to consider as a whole.

This requires a notably fluid style of performance, through which Smith appears as a kind of ninja of diverse characterization. As Robin Bernstein suggests: 'her simple shirt, trousers, bare feet, and slicked-back hair enhance her androgynous and racially indeterminate appearance and enable her to switch characters quickly across lines of race and gender' (2000: 123). The project is therefore to re-present rather than be a representative (in terms of inhabiting a subject position or taking sides). The dramaturgy underscores this, incorporating the audience into the position of Smith as neutral interviewer (experience-factor, truth-seeker), through the discursive functions of direct address (talking to the audience) and second-person positioning (addressing the spectator as 'you'). For Reinelt, the requirement this makes of the spectator – to reckon the various meanings that emerge from these different voices – 'is the most radical element of Smith's work ... the fundamental structural feature of Smith's work is the relationship of alterity under negotiation' (1996: 615).

I will suggest later that this ostensibly open and balanced approach – which seeks to find the rationale in every position – is one of the features that distinguishes Smith's work in the 1990s from performances in the twenty-first century amid a culture of overt separations and irreconcilable differences. For now, let's examine how Smith's form of documentary theatre was presented in the 1990s.

Fires in the Mirror

In 1992 Smith enjoyed a breakout hit with *Fires in the Mirror: Crown Heights Brooklyn and Other Identities*, followed a year later by *Twilight: Los Angeles, 1992*, both plays addressing the deep disturbance of race riots in East and West Coast America, respectively, and the practices and infrastructures of policing and judicial process that contributed to them. Given their closeness in time and topic, I shall consider both plays, starting with the first to be performed.

Critical and word-of-mouth responses to *Fires in the Mirror* were 'wildly enthusiastic' (Weatherston 2008: 191). The production won the Obie, Drama Desk and Lucille Lortel awards that year, and was a finalist for the 1992 Pulitzer Prize for Drama (whilst the Pulitzer committee subsequently decided that *Twilight*, the following year, was ineligible as a dramatic work since it was too closely dependent on 'the Real') (Weatherston 2008: 191). For all that, the MacArthur Foundation's citation on the occasion of its award to Smith of a 'genius grant' in 1996 included the accolade that Smith 'has created a new form of theater, a blend of theatrical art, social commentary, journalism and intimate reverie' (see Cohen and Koch 2007: 466). Smith subsequently received the 2012 National Humanities Medal from President Barack Obama for her 'portrayal of authentic American voices'.

Fires in the Mirror opened on 1 May 1992 at the Public Theatre in New York City (a TV version directed by George C. Wolfe, featuring Smith and produced by American Playhouse, was screened on 28 April 1993 on the PBS channel; for the playtext see Smith 2007). The play deals with the incidents and aftermath pertaining to four nights of rioting, from 19 to 22 August 1991, in the Crown Heights area of Brooklyn, New York City. The riots started after a car driven by a Jewish man jumped a traffic light, and the driver ran into another car and lost control, killing Gavin Cato, a Guyanese-American boy aged 7 and injuring the boy's cousin, Angela. The vehicle was one of three in convoy carrying the Lubavitcher Hasidic Rebbe, the spiritual leader of the Orthodox Jewish community. It was rumoured that the Hasidic-run ambulance that was first to arrive on the scene had helped the Jewish party and neglected the Black children. A group of Black youths attacked a Hasidic Jewish student, Yankel Rosenbaum, three hours later – he subsequently died of stab wounds. The principal engine of the riots, which lasted for three further days, was a series of attacks by Black protesters on the homes, vehicles and shops of Jewish people in the area (see Shapiro 2006).

In Autumn 1991 Smith conducted interviews with around a hundred people across the different communities in Crown Heights over a period of around eight days, and these formed the basis of her production. *Fires in the Mirror* was presented as a series of twenty-nine monologues that reprise the interview format – Smith performs the respective person, while the text also conjures her assumed presence as the interlocutor. This compounds the spectators' engagement, since they are to all intents and purposes placed as the explicit recipient of the talking (the second-person effect – the interviewee talks to 'you', the interviewer). The play is multivocal and multi-perspectival. It features artists and cultural commentators (including, for example, Ntozake Shange), civic authorities, community leaders, seemingly random members of the respective communities and relatives of the victims (Norman Rosenbaum, brother; and Carmel Cato, father). It circles around the events that started the riot and opens out into a form of ethnographic expansion concerning the lived lives of the communities, and reflection upon longer histories of oppression, enslavement and genocide.

As Cohen and Koch observe, Smith arranges the monologues 'for maximum revelation of individual complexity. She places Minister [Conrad] Mohammed's official declaration of Black chosen-ness and African American victimization after [Letty Cottin] Pogrebin's personal account of a family member who suffered the ravages of the Holocaust' (2007: 32).

FIGURE 2 *Billy Rose Theatre Division, The New York Public Library. Actress Anna Deavere Smith in a scene from the NY Shakespeare Festival production of the play* Fires in the Mirror. *The New York Public Library Digital Collections. 1992. https://digitalcollections. nypl.org/items/e1f26420-4bfd-0136-9f4c-0b741f361738*

The textual organization, then, invites the spectator to recognize both the historic oppression of enslaved African people and the drastic discrimination suffered by Jews under the Nazis. The implicit construction is that the violence of prejudice is a part of the deep history of the respective groups, without Smith appearing to promote one over the other. That said, cultural distinction is brought to the fore. Some interviewees reflect on their Blackness, for example, including the African American playwright and director George C. Wolfe:

You know what I mean.
That I was extraordinary as long as I was Black.
But I am – not – going – to place myself

(Pause)
in relationship to your whiteness.

(Smith 2007: 474)

An 'anonymous girl', described in the stage direction as 'a teenage Black girl of Haitian descent', says:

When I look at my parents,
That's how I knew I was Black.
Look at my skin.
You Black?
Black is beautiful.

(2007: 477)

In her published text, Smith includes stage directions that sometimes reflect upon the context in which the interview was undertaken. For example, the second monologue is that of an anonymous Lubavitcher woman:

(This interview was actually done on the phone. Based on what she told me she was doing, and on the three visits I had made to her home for other interviews, I devised this physical scene. A Lubavitcher woman, in a wig, and loose-fitting clothes. She is in her mid-thirties. She is folding clothes. There are several children around. Three boys of different ages are lying together on the couch. The oldest is reading to the younger two. A teen-age girl with long hair, a button-down-collar shirt, and skirt is sweeping the floor.)

(2007: 471)

These instances focus on the experience and expression of being Black, and the texture of daily life in a specifically Jewish household. Taken together they typify Smith's approach, to present a curated representation of actuality, edited to develop particular themes.

The play's effect is partly in the weaving that it performs of macro-historical reference and micro-cultural observation; and its deliberate presentation of what we might call *cultural texture*. By this I mean that it is important to the dramaturgical structure that no single voice predominates, and that the contradictions of various situated perspectives are corralled together (I shall explore this further when discussing *Twilight: Los Angeles, 1992*, below). The play mobilizes various authenticating strategies – the basis in individual interviews, the re-presentation of utterance with a scrupulous attention to accurate sonic replication, the choice of significant items of costume and props to convey individual specificity. However, it also deliberately theatricalizes its procedure, partly through the virtuosic aspect of Smith's performance (with all twenty-six characters under her belt), and partly through the dramatic flow of the piece, stitching its multifarious referential world as one cameo follows another. It is evidently edited, but in a manner that demonstrates tactical fullness rather than exclusion – the speeches are curated to include the pauses, repetitions and banalities of spoken exchange. This is an actualizing ploy; but is also part of the presentation of cultural texture as something that is lived, felt, inhabited – manifested through gesture, deportment, dress and utterance. The dramatic strategy is thereby rhetorical, gathering a deliberately disparate set of voices (people) in order to stage *speaking* as the substrate of lived experience. The focus is rather less on the journey of any one individual, and rather more on a plurality of individual sensibilities within demarcated cultural groups. This is perhaps a harbinger of a post-truth era. These are different truths, in a contested field. (See Kondo 2000: 96–8 for a discussion of this mode of performance as an overt resistance to racism.)

In Part One of Tony Kushner's play *Angels in America* (1991) Rabbi Isidor Chemelwitz describes the United States as 'the melting pot where nothing melted' (Kushner [1992] 2007: 16). This is a wry remark upon specifically American limits to multiculturalism, but it also shares a postmodern moment and sensibility with Smith's plays – decentred (albeit that Smith's work is arranged around the central performer), multivocal, relativist. We have moved from the linear narration of *In Spite of Everything!*, looking to make sense of a complicated series of events within a coherent narrative, to a deliberately open-ended, unresolved presentation of difference in speaking. Dramaturgically, what's brought to the fore and managed as a structuring principle is, precisely, plurality.

Twilight: Los Angeles, 1992

The same principle applies in Smith's next piece of documentary theatre, which responded to a set of riots on America's other coast. On 3 March 1991 Rodney G. King, a Black man, was beaten by four white police officers, while nineteen other officers stood by. The assault was videoed by George Holliday, and the 82-second recording circulated to news media. The four police officers were charged with using excessive force. The pre-trial proceedings began in Los Angeles County, but the trial proper was moved to Simi Valley, 'a conservative, largely white community in neighboring Ventura County, where a considerable number of police officers lived' (Smith 2011: 136). The trial ran from 4 March to 29 April 1992. Its outcome was the acquittal of the officers. Holliday's tape, in itself, wasn't the trigger for the riots but it provided an evidential record of the beating, meaning that the explosion of anger and anguish upon the verdict of the trial was surely inevitable. The rioting lasted for three days, and by the third President George Bush had ordered the deployment of 4,000 troops, amid reports that forty people had been killed, more than 1,500 injured and 3,700 fires started (see Taylor and Sanchez 1992; fifty-eight people were killed in all [Forsyth 2009: 150]). On 2 May 1992 Bush declared Los Angeles a disaster area.

The extent, nature and ferocity of the rioting caught civic authorities and commentators by surprise, as Mark Baldassare summarizes:

No one had expected that a jury viewing this tape would find the four police officers to be not guilty of using excessive force against Rodney King. The Los Angeles Police Department was unprepared when the personal shock over the trial outcome turned into angry and violent crowd behavior. Koreans did not seem to anticipate that the black rage against the white establishment would be diverted into looting their grocery stores and burning their small businesses. City officials, the police and local merchants did not expect Hispanic immigrants ... to be found in large numbers among the participants in the rioting and looting.
([1994] 2019: 2–3)[2]

Following the riots, Smith was commissioned by Gordon Davidson, artistic director of the Mark Taper Forum in Los Angeles, to make a one-woman show. In the manner employed in making *Fires in the Mirror*, Smith interviewed around 200 individuals, mostly face-to-face but sometimes by telephone, with an audio-recording (and sometimes a video recording) of the meeting. She used the transcripts to piece together a theatre show, working with a multiracial team of dramaturgs, featuring around twenty-five interviewees in the staged production. The show opened on 23 May 1993 at the Mark Taper Forum. Smith describes it as 'the product of my search for the character of Los Angeles in the wake of the initial Rodney King verdict' (1994: xvii).[3]

As with *Fires in the Mirror*, the individuals appear in series, one after the other, reverberating their various difference and overlaps. Since the testimonies depend upon individual recall, they tend to foreground personal implications and feelings rather than establishing a common narrative. This kind of documentary theatre, then, privileges felt experience. In that respect, it sits within an ideological commitment to the individual as the central gathering point of significance, which is partly why it is important to Smith's project to be ostensibly even-handed in presenting the range of interviewees. For example, Smith includes a section featuring her interview with Daryl Gates, former Chief of the Los Angeles Police Department, who was widely criticized for tactical decisions concerning his management of the police service prior to the riots and his actions in their aftermath. Gates says:

> and I swear
> I am the symbol
> of police oppression
> in the United States,
> if not the world.
> I am.
> Me!
> ...
> and it's a tough thing to deal with,
> a very tough thing.
>
> (Smith 1994: 185–6)

One of the jurors in the trial (figured in the playtext as 'Anonymous man') describes being doorstepped by a television journalist after the verdict was announced, having TV cameras trained on his house and seeing the value of his house published in the *New York Times* (he describes this as an invasion of privacy, whilst the account might lead one to reflect upon the newspaper's agenda to indicate the demographic of the members of the jury). He describes watching TV as both Tom Bradley (the Mayor of Los Angeles) and US President George Bush condemned the outcome of the trial, and goes on to say:

> One of the most disturbing things, and a lot of the jurors said that
> the thing that bothered them that they received in the mail more
> than anything else,
> more than the threats, was a letter from the KKK saying,
> "We support you, and if you need our help, if you want to join

our organization,
we'd welcome you into our fold."
And we all just were:
No, oh!
God!

(Smith 1994: 73)

These re-presentations – the powerful white chief of police, the anonymous juror inhabiting a place of white privilege – share experiences that are upsetting and perhaps even traumatic for the individuals concerned. As played out by an African American woman, doubly distinct from her subjects by way of both race and gender, they become additionally pointed. This returns us to the matter of Smith's assumption of all the roles. According to Dorinne Kondo, one of the dramaturgs on the piece, 'There is something astonishing and thought-provoking in seeing a person of one race and gender "don" the characteristics of so many who are "others" along so many different axes' (Kondo 2000: 82). I suggest that this applies with greater acuity in that, as a Black woman, Smith inhabits a cultural position that is doubly disprivileged, meaning that her appropriation of the 'other' performs a sharper sort of redress.

There is a pervasive layering of irony, too, and this is inherent to the dramaturgical structure. For Bernstein (not necessarily referring to the excerpts I have quoted above), 'Smith's black, female body portraying racist white men constituted a spectacular feat of compassion' (2000: 130). It also puts the person and their utterance in the dock. The Black woman chooses to voice the testimony of white power, which is placed alongside and equivalent to testimony from Black witnesses and indeed a range of individuals in various socio-cultural positions. Discourse therefore melts and bends – power does not necessarily reside in any one place (unless, for a moment, with the author and performer), nor does anybody (at least, anybody presented here) go unheard. Arjomand encapsulates a widely held critical perspective on this procedure: 'Smith's work does not stop at revealing

FIGURE 3 *Billy Rose Theatre Division, The New York Public Library. Actress Anna Deavere Smith in a publicity shot from the one-person play* Twilight: Los Angeles, 1992 *(New York). The New York Public Library Digital Collections. 1994.* https://digitalcollections.nypl.org/items/1eac1080-89fb-0132-969a-58d385a7b928

multiple voices and perspectives. It shows that the truth of an event emerges *through* these multiple perspectives, not *despite* them' (2018: 178, original emphasis).

The effect is to lay out a texture of personal *affectedness* – I mean the term as a compound to denote its gearing around affect (the things that the subject feels), and simultaneously around the impact of the events at the level of the person. The traumatic wound within the civil arena that the Rodney King case represents is felt within and by specific individuals. One feature of this dramatic texture, this weaving of the individual into the event, is a form of rejoining with history. It's perhaps a truism to say that events depicted in the news can appear remote from viewers, even when we are invested in or moved by them. The tapestry of reflective testimonies returns the individual to the event as an implicated subject. Consider the account of Elvira Evers, a cashier for the Canteen Corporation, who was pregnant at the time of the riots and shot in the stomach by a stray bullet. She recalls her conversation with her friend Frances:

> She say, "Lay down there. Let me call St. Francis and tell them that
> you been shot
> and to send an ambulance."
> And she say,
> "Why you?
> You don't mess with none of those people.
> Why they have to shoot you?"
>
> (Smith 1994: 119)

Individuals express their bemusement, their sense of the suddenness and specific peculiarity of what happened to them. Reginald Denny, a white man who was beaten in the riots by a man wielding a large canister, reflects that:

> what everyone thought was a fire extinguisher
> I got clubbed with,
> it was a bottle of oxygen,
> 'cause the guy had medical supplies [in the boot of his vehicle].
>
> (Smith 1994: 104)

The mode of recollection and its presentation in performance – and not least, the suffusion of dramatic irony that arises – produce a layering of time specific to this form of documentary drama. It also puts some emphasis on otherwise banal details, and I shall reflect on this further when discussing *The Colour of Justice*, below. Suffice to say here that there is a threefold intersection of 'the present': firstly there is the present moment of the initial event (the Denny beating, say); secondly there is its moment of recollection by the subject; and thirdly the moment of performance by Smith to a co-present audience, which reprises the second 'present' and recalls the first. A sub-theme concerning the interrelation of time, history and change runs through the piece. The writer Mike Davies, for example, one of Smith's interviewees, reflects on a previous era of civil rights development (I presume the 1960s and 1970s) in which 'black kids can be surfers too', and what's depicted as a downward spiral towards the 1990s where 'The beaches are patrolled by helicopters … [and] It's illegal to sleep on the, the beach anymore' (Smith 1994: 30, 31). Some of the testimony takes the spectator back to behind-the-scenes moments from the hot centre of the events. Angela King, Rodney King's aunt, says of King's beating:

> He couldn't talk,
> just "Der, der, der."
> I said, Goddam!
> I was right here
> when it happened.
> You want me to tell it?
> Ah …
> *(She starts crying;*
> *she makes about seven sobs)*
>
> (Smith 1994: 55)

Again, the effect is a form of temporal doubling and affective expansion, folding Angela King's recollection into the twin moments of lived distress during the interview and Smith's performance inhabiting its physical signs. And some of the testimony is directly thematic and lays out position statements (with which the audience is invited to agree or disagree). Theresa Allison, for example – described in the playtext as 'Founder of Mothers Reclaiming Our Children (Mothers ROC) Mother of gang truce architect Dewayne Holmes' (Smith 1994: 32) says:

> These police officers are just like you and I.
> Take that damn uniform off 'em,
> they the same as you and I.

Why do they have so much power?
Why does the system work for them?
Where can we go
to get the justice that they have?
Ts tuh!
Where? *(crying)*

(Smith 1994: 39)

An expression of anger and frustration articulates the lived experience of systemic injustice and structural discrimination. The combination of monologues deliberately pluralizes a scene; but it also serves to layer themes and interrelations and locate these in the experience of individuals. This makes for a complex (if open-ended) historicizing, that does not present a summative position on the events but circulates them as a kind of living document of distress and desire, framed in a postmodern aesthetics of inclusive relativism. Cherise Smith articulates the tensions in play. On the one hand, 'The liminality proffered in the performances reads as a leftist, humanist, integrationist fantasy that shades towards the neoconservative projects of colorblindness and postidentity' (2011: 19). And on the other hand, the various embodiments that Smith presents 'enable one to see that movements, behaviors, language, and signs are not "natural" parts of identity but learned actions and performances' (19).

The individual inhabits a shifting cultural landscape – one that is sometimes made more visible through performance. To this end, we can situate Smith's work in a longer tradition of American monologue performance, ranging from the oral history presentations by Studs Terkel (particularly between the 1950s and 1980s) to the autobiographical performances of Spalding Gray in the 1980s and 1990s, to Eric Bogosian's performance monologues over the last two decades of the twentieth century. Eddie Paterson argues that Smith's work 'extends the tradition of the monologue as a form of activist speech that highlights racial tension in American society – from Sojourner Truth to Frederick Douglass to Malcolm

X to Jesse Jackson' (2015: 104–5). We might connect this onwards with rap and hip hop. If this suggests a rather male lineage (Truth and female rappers excepted), Smith's work can also be located within a history of female solo presentation that might include the live performances of writer Maya Angelou, and Amanda Gorman's reading of her own poem, 'The Hill We Climb', at the inauguration ceremony for President Joe Biden in 2021. A slightly different reference point is provided by Adrienne Kennedy's one-act play *Funnyhouse of a Negro* (1964), 'with its quick-changing, one-woman virtuosity' exploring the identity slippages of a mixed-race woman (Winstein-Hibbs 2021: 817, referring to Debby Thompson 2003: 128). In his account of autobiographical performance, Marvin Carlson situates female artists such as Ruth Draper and Beatrice Herford in 'the stage monologue tradition, very important in America' (both performed in the United States in the first half of the twentieth century); and discusses Suzanne Lacy's work in the late 1970s and Whoopi Goldberg's *Direct from Broadway* show (1985), in which Goldberg presented a series of dramatic monologues (see Carlson 1996: 603). Smith joins with a considerable lineage, then, although she refunctions this through the rubric of documentary performance. As Rosemary Weatherston suggests, 'Unlike Gray, she did not recount and enact experiences from her own life, but from the lives of others … unlike Goldberg, these others were not fictional characters, they were living individuals' (Weatherston 2008: 192). And it's here that documentary theatre joins the actual with the experiential, in a procession of individual accounts. Smith's approach to this – through a journalistic interview process factored into a virtuosic set of performances – seeks to produce understanding about a massively impactful civic event through the accumulation of witness and testimony. We turn next to a production in the UK that did something very similar, but through different dramaturgical means.

The Colour of Justice – the context

The Colour of Justice (1999) presented scenes from a tribunal chaired by Sir William Macpherson inquiring into the police investigation into the murder of a young Black man. Let's deal first with the now well-known events reflected upon in the inquiry, and the outcome of the inquiry itself, before we turn to the play.

On 22 April 1993 Stephen Lawrence, aged 18, was stabbed to death. He and his friend Duwayne Brooks had been waiting for a bus in Eltham, south-east London, when a group of young white men attacked them and ran off. Brooks realized that his friend was hurt and called an ambulance from a phone box. A police control car was the first of the emergency services on the scene. Lawrence was taken to the nearby Brook General Hospital but was pronounced dead on arrival, having lost copious amounts of blood due to stab wounds to his arm and chest. The following day, a letter giving the names of a group of suspects was left in a phone box. Another anonymous note naming the suspects was left on the windscreen of a police patrol car. Three of the group, Gary Dobson and brothers Neil and Jamie Acourt, were arrested on 7 May, fifteen days after the murder. Luke Knight was arrested after a further three days. Duwayne Brooks identified Neil Acourt and Knight in identity parades. On 29 July the Crown Prosecution Service dropped the case because the evidence presented by Brooks was not deemed to be sufficient (the Macpherson Report determined that this was indeed the only route available to the judge at the time). The five suspects (including David Norris, who was also in custody) were released.

In August 1993 Detective Chief Superintendent John Barker conducted an internal review on behalf of the Metropolitan Police into the handling of the case, concluding that the officers had followed correct procedure. Macpherson found the findings of this review 'flawed and indefensible' and said that there could be 'no excuses for such a series of errors, failures, and lack of direction and control' as evidenced in the conduct of the case (1999: 368). A second inquiry conducted in 1994 by former Detective Superintendent William Mellish was, according to Macpherson, 'managed with imagination and skill' (368), but by that point no new evidence was forthcoming. In April 1995 a private prosecution brought by the Lawrence family began. The case fell through when the judge advised that the identification evidence of Duwayne Brooks could not be put to the jury since a statement from Detective Superintendent Crowley, who had accompanied Brooks to the identifications, called it into question (Crowley said that Brooks had indicated that he had received helpful information concerning identifications before the parade; Brooks disputed this account).

On 14 February 1997 the *Daily Mail* ran a one-word headline, 'Murderers' over the pictures of the five suspects, with the sub-head 'The Mail accuses these men of killing. If we are wrong, let them sue us'. (The men never did. The newspaper repeated the front page on 27 July 2006. The matter raises questions concerning the tactics and effect of media interventions that I won't go into here but mention because they are part of the extraordinary scope of this case.) In July 1997 the then Home Secretary, Jack Straw, ordered a judicial public inquiry, under Sir William Macpherson, to start after the submission (in December 1997, as it turned out) of a report commissioned by the Police Complaints Authority and undertaken by the Kent Constabulary. The Kent Report found fault with many aspects of the previous Metropolitan Police internal review.[4]

Macpherson's Inquiry was exhaustive, its report compendious – albeit that it might be seen as succinct compared with some in the genre (Cathcart 2012: 982) – and its outcome seismic in relation to the activities of the police, legal process and the picture it affirmed of social relations in the UK. The rigour and extent of the inquiry's report, with its categorical condemnation of the Metropolitan Police, marked a watershed that seemed at least as significant as that drawn by the Scarman Report of 1981 addressing the Brixton Riots of that year. (Lord Scarman's report led to the establishment of the Police Complaints Authority in 1985; Macpherson found that many of Scarman's recommendations relating to the police had not been followed up.) Among its recommendations, the Macpherson Report advised that the 'double jeopardy' law (by which an individual judged not guilty of an offence could not be tried again for the same crime) should be repealed. The law was partially amended in the Criminal Justice Act 2003 with effect from April 2005. Two of the five men suspected of Lawrence's murder, Gary Dobson and David Norris, were convicted on 3 January 2012 on the basis of the presentation of new evidence, after the case was retried. In addition, in consequence of the Report, the Race Relations Act 1976 was amended by the Race Relations (Amendment) Act 2000 (Dahl 2009: 128).

In the conclusion to his report, Macpherson makes the following withering assessment: 'The [Metropolitan Police] investigation was marred by a combination of professional incompetence, institutional racism and a failure of leadership by senior officers. A flawed MPS [Metropolitan Police Service] review failed to expose these inadequacies' (1999: 365). This charge of institutional racism had a particularly deep reverberation. Where Scarman found in 1985 that the Metropolitan Police Service was not institutionally racist, Macpherson arrived at a different conclusion fourteen years later. Macpherson defines the phenomenon as follows:

> 'Institutional Racism' consists of the collective failure of an organisation to provide an appropriate and professional service to people because of their colour, culture or ethnic origin. It can be seen or detected in processes, attitudes and behaviour which amount to discrimination through unwitting prejudice, ignorance, thoughtlessness, and racist stereotyping which disadvantage minority ethnic people.
>
> (1999: 369)

Much of this had already been assumed and articulated by many people over many years, but its formulation by the eminent chair of a public inquiry was a different matter. When Macpherson began his inquiry, the case had already ballooned into one that concerned race relations in the UK, the very function of policing in contemporary society, the competence and capability of the Metropolitan Police (charged with serving the notably diverse population of London), and the adequacy of the legal system with respect to the due process of justice. By the time he concluded it, he presented condemnation, a challenge and a lament with drastic clarity.

The Colour of Justice – the play

This, then, was the context for *The Colour of Justice*, first performed at the Tricycle Theatre, London, on 6 January 1999, directed by Nick Kent (with Susan Fletcher-Jones), from transcripts of the Macpherson Inquiry edited by Richard Norton-Taylor.[5]

When the production opened, Macpherson's report had not yet been published (it was released on 24 February 1999), so there was a sense of hot-off-the-press reportage to the show (albeit that the inquiry itself had lasted many months, with 69 days of public hearings that generated transcripts of over 11,000 pages) (Brittain et al. 2014: 292). It was the fourth in what became known as the 'Tribunal' series: plays presented between 1994 and 2012 by the Tricycle, under Nicolas Kent's artistic directorship, exploring matters at the rawer edges of public and socio-political interest.[6] *Half the Picture* was the first of these (1994, addressing the Scott 'arms to Iraq' inquiry), followed by *Nuremberg* (1996, reprising parts of the Nuremberg Trial of German Major War Criminals of 1945–6, on the occasion of its fiftieth anniversary) and *Srebrenica* (1996, addressing the International War Crimes Tribunal hearings at the Hague that year concerning Bosnian Serb leaders Radovan Karadžić and Ratko Mladić).

The form proved robust enough to encourage some modal development. *Guantanamo: 'Honor Bound to Defend Freedom'* (2004), for example, was put together from interviews conducted with five British former-detainees of the US-run internment camp, along with other statements in the public domain by political and judicial leaders in the United States and UK. *Called to Account* (2007) – pieced together from interviews conducted with individuals (lawyers, members of parliament, academics) for the purpose of the production – envisages a hearing concerning an indictment of British Prime Minister Tony Blair for the crime of aggression in relation to the invasion of Iraq in 2003. These more adventurous excursions underpin the central premise of the tribunal series as a whole: verbatim utterances from people who have skin in the game, packaged and reprised for a theatre audience, are variously compelling and revealing. What's more, they present the complexities of a matter in a way that reveals dimensions that might otherwise remain obscure. Kent, at least, had this revelatory mission in mind from the outset. He says of *Half the Picture*: 'you had a public inquiry, that was actually not seen by the public, because it wasn't televised, it wasn't on the net, and it was only reported in segments that the journalist chose to write about ... So you had a very censored version' (Brittain et al. 2014: 9).

For all that this suggests a project of enlightenment, the tribunal plays entailed an extraordinary job of textual selection and slashing. Most involved the *Guardian* journalist Richard Norton-Taylor as a kind of curator-dramaturg-editor, deciding which individual testimonies would be used and how much of each would be presented. As Kent observes, '[the individuals] become emblematic to some extent ... So you've got to find the best one that then encapsulates the best story' (Brittain et al. 2014: 14). As we shall see, this underlying concern with clarity of narration was important to the production team, although it had already been demonstrated elsewhere. By the time of *The Colour of Justice*, a theatrical form based on tribunal and trial proceedings was already familiar from productions such as Hochhuth's *The Deputy* (1963) and Weiss's *The Investigation* (1965), which Piscator worked on as we saw in the previous chapter. Kent remarks that he was influenced by Eric Bentley's *Are You Now or Have You Ever Been?* (1993, about the McCarthy Hearings on un-American activities) and the TV drama reconstruction of the inquiry into the death in custody of South African Black activist Steve Biko (*The Biko Inquest*, United British Artists, 1984) (Brittain et al. 2014: 5). The Tricycle series wasn't exactly defining a new kind of theatre, then, but it did road-test and refine an established mode. In so doing, it represents a powerful confluence of civic proceedings and performance that gave a new vigour to reality-trend political theatre in the 1990s and early twenty-first century (and I shall say a little more about this towards the end of this chapter).

The play presents a litany of instances of incompetence or malpractice on the part of police officers. While Stephen Lawrence was bleeding to death, the officers who attended the scene failed to identify the nature of his injury and did not seek to apply first aid (Norton-Taylor 2014: 304; unless otherwise indicated, page references in this section refer to this edition). A photographer was assigned to undertake surveillance of the Acourts' house. Before he had set up his camera, in the words of Edmund Lawson QC (Counsel to the inquiry), 'he saw somebody leaving their house with what appeared to be clothing in a bin bag, get into a car and clear off. He made no report at the time of either of these events' (306). The search of the locale, on the night of the murder, was undertaken by police who included a detachment of officers who had one rechargeable torch between them (330). The officers undertaking the initial house-to-house investigation were not told the names of the suspects, which had quickly been made available to the police (332–3).

This might all be straightforward ineptitude. Worse, perhaps, is the implication of deliberate casualness at best, and more likely obfuscation. All the 'tag sheets' that detail the movements of the respective police vehicles used that night had gone missing by the time of the inquiry (334). Shortly after the murder an anonymous man who became known as James Grant passed information to the police. The record of interviews with him went missing. It turns out that Grant had found a witness on a bus who could describe the stabbing, and effectively names Neil Acourt and Norris. The information was provided on 27 April. The person on the bus was seen by the police on 19 May. It later became clear that one of the police officers involved in the case was 'consorting' with Clifford Norris, the father of one of the suspects and wanted, at the time, for drug importation (388). The officer concerned was put in charge of Brooks during part of the time that Brooks was involved in the police enquiries.

Faced with facts of this nature, some of the exchanges are grimly comic. For example, Edmund Lawson QC asks Inspector Groves about his record and recollection of the events of the evening of the murder.

> LAWSON: I understand, is this correct, that you have no surviving notes?
> GROVES: No sir, I have not.
> LAWSON: There was a reference to you having a clipboard at the scene?
> GROVES: I still have the clipboard. I don't have any notes. (344–5)

Michael Mansfield QC (Counsel for the Lawrence family) interviews former Detective Sergeant John Davidson about his meetings with the informant known as Grant:

> MANSFIELD: There is in fact absolutely no record, is there, in relation to any of the meetings – and there are quite a number of them – that you had with this man?
> DAVIDSON: That's correct, sir.
> MANSFIELD: Why not?
> DAVIDSON: The docket went missing, sir. (358)

If you were writing a cheap comedy about a bumbling police service, you could hardly script anything more suitable than this. However, Mansfield enlarges the accusation:

> MANSFIELD: To put it bluntly, you really did not want this informant's material to be effectively followed up. Do you follow the point?

Benedict Feldman argues that the Tricycle's tribunal plays 'have developed new ways of staging and interrogating culpability, redirecting the spectator's attention away from the victim to those responsible for his or her victimization' (Feldman 2021: 608). He elaborates the case with reference to Hannah Arendt's critique of the trial of the Nazi Adolf Eichmann: 'The Tribunal Theatre succeeds, where according to Arendt the trial of Eichmann failed, to place the banality of modern, bureaucratic wrongdoing center stage' (601).

Banality can be both risible and awful, simultaneously. What kind of theatre is this; and, to ask the question slightly differently, how does it work (if it does) theatrically?

Theatre and anti-theatre

In her account of verbatim theatre in the UK either side of the new millennium, Catherine Rees suggests that the tribunal plays at the Tricycle 'offered political theatre a new and radically anti-theatrical aesthetic … the plays did much to undermine a sense of theatricality; they played with the house lights still up and the cast took no curtain calls' (2019: 308, 311). For Mary Karen Dahl, 'The performance mode was understated. One reviewer [Benedict Nightingale in the *Times*] described it as "acting-that-isn't-acting"' (2009: 141). What was this anti-theatre with its non-acting?

First, it was very much still theatre, perhaps even in a rather familiar naturalistic mode. The tribunal plays were typically presented in a conventional theatrical end-on format, with the spectators watching the action arranged on stage in front

FIGURE 4 *A scene from* The Colour of Justice, *Tricycle Theatre, showing the layout of the courtroom. Photo © Tristram Kenton.*

of them. The scenic design replicated the look and feel of the courtroom or tribunal room – the chair of the proceedings seated broadly in the centre upstage, or on a raised platform; tables and witness stand in keeping with the business at hand; and various paraphernalia of the media management of the room, with its use of microphones to amplify testimony, stenographers to capture the spoken word, and screens to display relevant documents. Stoller remarks upon the fidelity of the production to its source material, and notes that 'The accurate re-creation extends to the mise-en-scène: the computers, the rows of desks, the ring binders, lawyers whispering to each other, and people walking in and out' (2013: 297). According to Valerie Kaneko-Lucas, '*The Colour of Justice* creates the ambiance of an English courtroom, where the conventions of professional comportment ask the witness to "report" rather than "relive" the event, keeping an aesthetic distance from the material' (2007: 268). This helps to explain the apparent non-acting of the actors, who typically ask questions or respond in a judicial question-and-answer format, rather than play out more casual exchanges. In his discussion with Kent, Norton-Taylor and Slovo towards the beginning of the edition of collected tribunal plays, David Edgar asks about 'the obvious problems as well as the delights of mimicry' (thinking of the appearance in the plays of major figures in political life including Margaret Thatcher, Michael Heseltine and Alastair Campbell). 'Yes, we always said less is more' replies Kent. 'We tried to get to the essence of what the scene was about' (Brittain et al. 2014: 19). This mode of performance is a little different from that of Anna Deavere Smith. There is indeed some doubling of different characters by some actors in various plays in the series, but only for purposes of exigency. Actors are cast according to the ethnicity of the individuals they play. Nor is there the bravura scope of performance, including the minutely observed attempt to replicate, that we saw in Smith's one-person productions. The audience is invited to hear the utterance of the person rather than admire the performance of the actor.

The courtroom premise supports this focus on a transaction with facts, evidence, individual recollection and personal agency. The production is therefore notably epistemic, concerned with the process by which events and perspectives are understood and validated. The courtroom itself is an engine for knowledge and adjudication, organized spatially and functionally for speaking and hearing. If it is arranged around structures of agonistic exchange (to put it in a way that reminds us of the staged discourse of Greek tragedy), with an individual on one side of the stage asking questions of an individual on the other side, it also asks the spectator to come to their own judgement about the matters presented. As Kaneko-Lucas suggests, 'In form as well as content, these plays embrace an aesthetic which engages the spectator as witness and as judge' (2007: 265). The accounts of individuals must be sifted. Perspective accumulates.

What emerges is a matrix of interconnectedness; and layers of time that enforce both sequence and consequence on the one hand, and non-linear interrelationships on the other. This applies in the original inquiry, which was unpacked over weeks and months, concerned events that happened within a chronology, and required extensive connection of evidence from different parties in order to arrive at a view; but also in terms of the theatrical experience in the face of the production. For my part, having seen several of the tribunal shows, I find the format absorbing for its presentation of facets and fragments, which offer an almost puzzle-like pleasure in consolidation; and affecting in its moments of revelation and recognition. Much of this derives from what we might think of as the inherent theatricality of the actual courtroom in the first place. In his account of the original proceedings in the Macpherson Inquiry, Brian Cathcart observes that:

> Half of the public gallery at the inquiry, the half with the better view, faced across the room towards the witness box ... During police evidence, and particularly when [Stephen] Kamlish [Counsel to the Lawrence family] or Mansfield were tying officers in knots, the audience was plainly absorbed by the spectacle and laughter or groans would greet some of the more unexpected answers.
>
> (2012: 793)

Something similar occurs in the theatre with the restaging of some of these interviews. In slightly different vein, Cathcart reflects upon the moment after a lunch break when Macpherson, having listened in the morning session to the testimony of John Barker (author of the first and eventually discredited Metropolitan Police review), says that he will make a statement to the chamber on behalf of his advisers and himself. '[W]e feel we ought to indicate that this [Barker's] review is likely to be regarded by us as indefensible for what must be obvious reasons in these circumstances,' Macpherson announces. Cathcart reflects that 'It was an extraordinary moment. Here was a former senior officer at Scotland Yard, a former head of the Flying Squad, being dismissed by the inquiry chairman as an unreliable witness' (2012: 840).

Such extraordinary moments then reverberate in the theatre production. The layering of time is important here, and this feature is underpinned by the authenticity effects of the production – the fidelity to the transcripts, the effort to replicate rather than embellish, the hyper-realist *mise en scène*. This gives us an apparently direct and unfiltered access to the tribunal proceedings, so that the spectator can envisage how this played out in its originary moments. The tribunal, in all its historical actuality, is the source of the production. And yet the tribunal itself is concerned with events (themselves actual) that took place in the past, and through their testimonies the witnesses take themselves (and thereby the spectators) to the moments of action, reaction and decision that occurred as part of the fabric of the case in question. This situates the event in time past, twice removed (from the play in the present and the tribunal in the past); but with its significance doubled through the attention of deliberate scrutiny and recall of both tribunal and play. And, moreover, through the agency of performance – for the event (put on a plate, so to speak) inhabits the present experience of the spectator. It's here that the tribunal mode is especially theatrical (rather than anti-theatrical) in its operation. Kent observes that 'We made a rule that we would never ever jump the chronology. We'd always take witnesses in the order in which they appeared in the Inquiry' (Brittain et al. 2014: 13). This decision provides a form of linear backbone to the play – a narrative drive, indeed – whilst it negotiates non-linear connections across incidents (moments) and processes (durations). If I can interpellate an audience in the first person: we laugh at inapt or inept answers, we are distressed at upsetting descriptions and revelations, we want to know what happened, and we engage with the accumulative implications of the matter. Such engagement concerns us with the individuals involved, wider socio-civic consequences, and our own involvement as a kind of sampler, sifter and sense-maker. And if this suggests that the whole thing is about arriving at understanding, the efficacy of the work resides as much in its operation as a machine for feeling. The spectator navigates (is positioned across) differential layers of time and place, through the ostensibly static setting of the tribunal room, precisely to have an affective experience in the face of the production of knowledge. Indeed, this was affirmed in the minute's silence in memory of Stephen Lawrence and (as Macpherson observes) 'the courage of his parents' (Norton-Taylor 2014: 415) that ends the play – taking its cue from the minute's silence with which Macpherson ended the inquiry proceedings.

Racism and testimony

In its account of a racist murder and the instruments of systemic racism, how does *The Colour of Justice* stage testimony that concerns racism? The play was produced by a largely white team – director Kent (with Surian Fletcher-Jones), writer Norton-Taylor, designer Bunny Christie. It describes proceedings that are overseen by a white former judge (Macpherson), with leading Counsel who are white (Lawson, Mansfield and Gompertz), and whose senior officers providing testimony (the respective policemen) are white. (We note that all these figures, Fletcher-Jones and Christie apart, are also male.) I'm not necessarily suggesting that Black experience can only be expressed by Black writers, directors and voices, but noting here that (against a racialized norm that privileges whiteness) it emerges as a refiguring of perspective in the inquiry and is reprised by a theatre production machinery that isn't notably diverse. What's dramatized, then, is a form of challenge from within – a government-commissioned process (the public judicial inquiry) holding a part of the establishment to account, replayed and funnelled through the institution of theatre (itself subject to inequities). Amid the layers of power transaction here, both inquiry and play perform a holding-to-account.

The Tricycle could in any case claim a track record for addressing the concerns and experiences of Black Londoners.

Writers to have their work featured at the theatre during Kent's tenure as artistic director include Michael Abensetts, Mustapha Matura, James Baldwin, August Wilson, Roy Williams, Winsome Pinnock, Alice Childress, Lynn Nottage, Kwame Kwei-Armah and Bola Agbaje (Stoller's chapter 'Black theatre at the Tricycle' addresses this history, largely through recollections of individuals involved in the respective productions: 2013: 73–187). Kaneko-Lucas notes drily that in 1999 'the Tricycle was one of only three producing theatres in England to have black representatives on their boards of trustees' (2007: 264).

We might think that this provides a rather more acceptable model of institutional competency with regard to issues concerning race.[7] The Tricycle's programming connects with a shift in focus in Black theatre productions over the period. Goddard suggests that the period of the Stephen Lawrence Inquiry 'coincides with a perceptible shift in the concerns of black British playwriting away from the diaspora themes of the 1980s and 1990s and into tackling urgent contemporary social issues in Britain today' (2015: 40; see also Brewer et al. 2015: 7; Peacock 2015: 154). In any case, the play (and indeed the proceedings) cannot help but foreground the issue of racism. There are two principal modes at work – one is the overt racism expressed by the suspects (notoriously captured when the police planted a surveillance camera in a flat belonging to one of them), the other the more subliminal and casual racism expressed through the actions, inactions and choices of the police officers. Much of the testimony concerns the latter.

For example, when Kamlish interviews Detective Constable Linda Holden, family liaison officer to the Lawrence family, it is clear that she doesn't see the bias in her actions and responses. Kamlish reprises the known details of the attack, including the use by one of the assailants of the n-word and the fact that the two men assaulted were not known to the attackers, and asks Holden what she thinks the motive for the attack was.

HOLDEN: I accept all the circumstances surrounding it and I know what you are saying but I can't say what was in the minds of those thugs that killed him. I don't know what their motive was. I can't answer that.
(Norton-Taylor 2014: 368)

Michael Mansfield frames the case in a way that reverberated with Macpherson's subsequent findings:

So much was missed by so many that deeper causes and forces must be considered. We suggest these forces relate to two main propositions. The first is that the victim was black and racism, both conscious and unconscious, permeated the investigation. Secondly, the fact that the perpetrators were white and were expecting some form of protection.
(Norton-Taylor 2014: 306)

This perspective is, in effect, dramatized in a testy exchange between Mansfield and Inspector Groves, which includes Groves's indication that he understood the initial call-out to the scene to concern a fight.

MANSFIELD: You see, the information that the inquiry has been told was effectively, an assault with an iron bar [misreported initially as the cause of the injuries to Lawrence], quite different to a fight. In other words, somebody being attacked. That was your information, Mr Groves?
GROVES: Sir, of course, I would agree with you.
MANSFIELD: You translated, I suggest to you, the information of an assault into: black man on pavement involved in fight. Is that a possibility?
GROVES: Of course that is a possibility, absolutely.
(Norton-Taylor 2014: 352)

The picture is rounded out in the testimonies of Stephen's parents. The statement of his father, Neville, is read out by

Martin Soorjoo (part of Mansfield's team). He tells of coming to England in 1960 aged 18, having served an apprenticeship as an upholsterer and being unable to find work. 'I believe this was because of racism. The racism that we experienced then was not as bad as that we now experience. In those days it was mostly verbal, not physical. The violence is much worse nowadays' (Norton-Taylor 2014: 342). Doreen Lawrence's statement, read out by Margo Boye-Anawoma, part of Mansfield's team, includes the following magisterial summation: 'If it wasn't racism what was it? Incompetence? Corruption? That only goes some way to explain … What went wrong? Something did. Their attitude tells me that it was racism' (393).

On the publication of the Macpherson Report on 24 February 1999, Home Secretary Jack Straw made a statement in the House of Commons to announce the findings and recommendations. Straw said 'The very process of the inquiry has opened all our eyes to what it is to be black or Asian in Britain today. And the inquiry process has revealed some fundamental truths about the nature of our society, about our relationships, one with the other' (in Cathcart 2012: 982). As Brewer et al. suggest, the intersection between Black experience and whiteness 'means that Black-defined Britishness involves not only the representation of a more authentic black identity, but also the deconstruction and refashioning of hegemonic whiteness in Britain' (2015: 7). The inquiry, its report and the subsequent play reveal the pervasiveness of this hegemony right at the heart of the institution most geared to protect the public, which turns out to be rather more attuned to protecting uninspected assumptions concerning the status quo.

Postscripts

The Tricycle tribunal plays helped provide the terms of engagement for a larger swell of verbatim and documentary-based dramas over this period (including for example, as mentioned in Chapter 1, *The Exonerated* [2000],

The Laramie Project [2000], *Talking to Terrorists* [2005], David Hare's verbatim-inflected plays and the productions of *Recorded Delivery*). This work gave a newly viable form to a renewed interest in socio-political controversies and processes – one that that seemed to access the realities involved as directly as possible. Did it thereby act as a witness to change? In their reflection upon the legacy of the Macpherson Report, a year after its publication, Marlow and Loveday suggest that 'The levers are in place. It is now up to chief officers to use them. Macpherson followed Scarman after eighteen years. The prospect of a similar condemnation in a couple of decades is too appalling to contemplate' (2000: 2).

Roll forward a couple of decades. On 21 March 2023 Baroness Louise Casey's excoriating report into the standards of behaviour and internal culture of the Metropolitan Police Service was published (Casey 2023). Casey's review was initiated by Dame Cressida Dick, Commissioner of the Metropolitan Police Service at the time, after the abduction and murder of Sarah Everard in South London in March 2021 by a serving police officer. Of the Casey Report's eight main conclusions, the first identifies 'systemic and fundamental problems in how the Met is run), while the seventh finds that discrimination is 'not dealt with and has become baked into the system' (Casey 2023: 11, 16) As Casey observes:

> Many of the issues raised by the Review are far from new. I make a finding of institutional racism, sexism and homophobia in the Met. Sir William Macpherson made the first of those findings in his inquiry into the racist murder of Stephen Lawrence as long ago as 1999. Many people have been raising grave concerns about the Met for much longer than that.
>
> (Casey 2023: 7)

Macpherson found the Metropolitan Police institutionally racist. Twenty-four years later, Casey adds misogyny and homophobia to the charge sheet.

Meanwhile in the United States, in a case that had grim parallels to that of Rodney King: on 7 January 2023 the Memphis Police Department released video footage (from body-camera and streetlamp camera footage) that showed the beating of 29-year-old Tyre Nichols by five policemen. The assault took place after the police had undertaken a traffic stop on Nichols' car. One of the officers had pulled him out, Nichols attempted to flee after being forced to the ground, and he was subsequently apprehended at an intersection. Nichols appears to offer no threat or resistance, and the assault is brutal and callous. Nichols died of his injuries on 10 January. Eight officers appear to stand around after the beating, offering no assistance to the stricken victim. Five of the officers were subsequently dismissed and on 26 January were charged 'with second-degree murder, aggravated assault, aggravated kidnapping, official misconduct and official oppression in the death of Nichols' (Bekiempis 2023). The five police officers were Black.

Since we are concerned with realities and their mediation, and with the future of the documentary topic as well as its past, it seems only proper to include this depressing update. In the next chapter I consider five productions that in different ways maintain a search for connection and recognition; and reflect upon newly obvious jeopardies to the truth (however you hold it).

4

Mediations and representations – multiple perspectives and practices: 2008 to 2023

In Chapter 1 we noted the emergence of 'post-truth' as a conceptual point of reference for culture and politics in the second decade of the twenty-first century. In his book *Post Truth: The New War on Truth and How to Fight Back*, Matthew D'Ancona presents a visceral lament in face of 'the infectious spread of pernicious relativism disguised as legitimate scepticism' (2017: 2) – the condition (among others) that led to the Leave vote in the UK's Brexit referendum in 2016 and the election of Donald Trump as US President later that year. D'Ancona is a journalist (an occupation that provides something of a sub-theme to this chapter) and deals with both phenomena with bitter attention to detail. Towards the start of the book he discusses the press conference on 21 January 2017 given by Sean Spicer, the newly installed White House press secretary, the day after the ceremony confirming Trump's inauguration. Reports in the press had compared the audience turnout unfavourably in comparison with that of Barack Obama's inauguration in 2009. Spicer told the gathered press corps that 'this was the largest audience to ever witness an inauguration, period' (in D'Ancona 2017: 12). D'Ancona describes the Trump administration's next steps in correcting the coverage.

> As angry as Spicer and his boss might be, their position was hilariously unsustainable. It fell to Kellyanne Conway, senior aide to the President, to find some way of squaring the epistemological circle, of reconciling bogus claim with photographic evidence. On NBC's *Meet the Press* the next day, Conway told Chuck Todd that there was a perfectly reasonable explanation: 'Don't be so overly dramatic about it, Chuck. You're saying it's a falsehood ... Sean Spicer, our press secretary, gave alternative facts to that.
>
> (2017: 13)

Here is the post-truth discourse of alternative facts and contestation about 'fake news', mobilized as part of a political programme to secure effects of power. A few pages later, D'Ancona cites Aaron Banks, the businessman who funded the Leave.EU campaign: 'The Remain campaign featured fact, fact, fact. It just doesn't work. You've got to connect with people emotionally. It's the Trump success' (in D'Ancona 2017: 17). D'Ancona goes on to report that 'In December 2016, an Ipsos poll for BuzzFeed of more than 3,000 Americans found that 75 per cent of those who saw fake news headlines judged them to be accurate ... All that matters is that the stories *feel* true; that they resonate' (2017: 53–4, original emphasis). This recalls Kelsey Jacobson's coinage 'real-ish', as we saw in Chapter 1, to denote the triumph of subjective perception over ontological certainty (2023: 11). As D'Ancona himself argues, much of the context for the defraying of shared agreements about matters of fact can be traced in the years and indeed decades prior to the plebiscitary outcomes of 2016. One tributary, paradoxically, is the anti-authoritarian work of postmodernism, which sought to decentre and destabilize fixed structures of power and authority. Relativizing was increasingly mainstreamed – in effect, my facts might well be different from yours. In any case, as we shall see in discussing the work that provides a focus for this chapter, the notion of the instability of the truth was already centre stage.

What do we make of documentary theatre practice amid this terrain where facts are viciously disputed, and parallel realities asserted? This chapter argues that documentary both concentrates and refracts as it moves into the new millennium; and that theatre-makers and performance practitioners find value precisely at the junction of fact and fiction, where truth is both sought and shown to be in jeopardy. Enabled by the ubiquitous recording and real-time dissemination of digital technologies and social media, *actuality* becomes setting, topic and focus of mediation. It is also valorized in some performance situations and undercut in others – and sometimes both at once. The older style of revelation and representation is supplanted by an encounter (for the spectator) with a particular context and its thematic reverberations. Meanwhile the growth of 'immersive' theatre and associated entertainment formats brings documentary's concerns with veracity, situated knowledge and affective engagement into a theatrical repertoire that (so to say) drops the spectator in it.

There are connections between this and a wider array of engagements with and through performance that provide the frisson of actuality within structures of entertainment. These include, for example, sports events where pleasure is mediated and replayed in relation to actual outcomes; and online games, including world-building, quest and 'shooter' formats that offer intensifications of pleasure in real-time exchanges. We also observe an extension of fact-oriented work across a range of artistic outputs and forms. To take the long-form novel: Hilary Mantel's trilogy focusing on Thomas Cromwell, a courtier in the time of Henry VIII, offers a pertinent example. Mantel tells Cromwell's story in a present-tense construction that both objectifies and subjectifies the narrative, performing the slippage across fact and fabrication that is so characteristic of cultural production in this period. It situates the reader within Cromwell's journey and perspective, whilst having all the appearance of close observation of his thoughts, actions and milieu – thereby offering a literary meld of felt experience (Cromwell's) and seemingly thick description suffused with detail of the Tudor age (Mantel 2009, 2012, 2020).[1] In the popular fiction market there is a slew of writing that ostensibly presents close-textured accounts of historical narratives. This attention to period detail – the warp and weft of apparent historical facticity – aligns with a broader and ongoing fascination with period costume drama on television and in film. Fictional treatments are only part of the nexus of work transacting with notions of actuality in popular entertainment. From reality game shows, to competition format shows featuring individuals undertaking challenges of various kinds, to 'makeover' shows, to travelogues, to revelatory autobiographical programmes, fact-based work demonstrates a cultural fascination with the circumstances and behaviour of individuals in specific (often theatricalized) environments. Indeed, the dramaturgical arrangement and narrative rhythm of such shows are precisely theatrical; and not least in their offer of pleasure through public manifestation of outcomes that are sometimes life-changing.

While documentary continues as a recognizable form in theatre, cinema and television, the business of exploring fact-based and (let's say) actual-person-based work has become pervasive as a cultural mode. Meanwhile the substrates of documentary – fact, reportage, verification – have been simultaneously undermined amid the fragmenting effects of divergent news outlets, the absolutist 'bubbles' of social media and large-scale civic and plebiscitary processes that have emphasized divisions in society and produced radical separation in what people believe to be true. To navigate documentary in this setting, let's consider the theatre production *Radio Muezzin* (2008), the podcast *Serial* (Season 2, 2015–16), the installation *Domo de Eŭropa Historio en Ekzilo* (*The House of European History in Exile*) (2013), the theatre/online production *The Wall* (2023) and the spoken-word performance *Even at the*

Risk (2022). Each reveal something about twenty-first-century approaches to documentary and, taken together, they open out into negotiations of national and individual identity at a point where these categories are under stress and contestation.

Radio Muezzin

Around the turn of the millennium, a German theatre company started developing work that gave rise to the term *Theater der Zeit* – 'theatre of the time', which we've come to know in English as 'reality trend' theatre. This is Rimini Protokoll, who formed in 2002 after its three directors (Helgard Haug, Stefan Kaegi and Daniel Wetzel) had left the Institute for Applied Theatre Studies at the Justus Liebeg University in Giessen, near Frankfurt, Germany.[2]

The work is variously venue-based, site-specific, perambulatory and nomadic; involves different media – including radio, video, theatrical presentation and installation; and includes texts of various kinds, from formal instructions, to schematic rubrics, to individual testimonies. The work also includes framing other events as theatre, notably in *Annual Shareholder's Meeting* (2008), in which the company secured tickets to the annual shareholder's meeting of the vehicle manufacturer Daimler and produced various satellite events and paraphernalia that treated the proceedings as a piece of staged performance; and *World Climate Change Conference* (2014/15), which entailed participants in theatres in Hamburg, Linz and Munich, where the company presented the piece, working through various discussions, negotiations and tactical positioning mapped against the issues and agenda of the international climate conference in Paris in December 2015.

The company, then, is interested in intersections between lived experience and aesthetic re-presentation (as distinct from representation); and registers of reality that move across the activities and experience of the individuals who are subject of the work, and the awareness of encounter of the members of the audience. There is a taste for innovation here – for example, in *Cargo Sofia-X* (2008) the audience sat in a container pulled by a lorry truck, listening to the conversation of two Bulgarian truck drivers about their work in cross-border commercial transit, while watching through the adapted side of the container as the lorry travelled around Tallinn, or Bordeaux, or Barcelona, or wherever the show happened to be; or at times watching video projected on a screen along the inside of the container. (The piece was also presented in and through other cities, as for example in *Cargo Congo-Lausanne* [2018] and *Cargo Shanghai-Friesland* [2022].) But this is also a body of work that sustains a longer avant-garde interest in escaping or emptying out 'established' modes of theatre (for example, to do with character-based dramatic narrative) and seeking means by which to 're-real' the performance. Hamilton points to the company's deliberate exposure of 'restricted, neglected or potentially unnoticed bodies and spaces as part of a larger flexible project dedicated to fresh affiliations and interconnection with the "real"' (2015: 73). Here, this reality drive is through a kind of *revelation* – the experiences of various groups whose lives the Rimini Protokoll spectators might not normally see (truck drivers, muezzin, train enthusiasts); and through a form of *verfremdung*, to use the Brechtian term, in which the audience is made aware of the processes by which the piece is presented. This means that the work typically revolves around interconnected poles: both theatrical production and social and locational context; multimodal mediation and audience reception; and a playful presentation of topic and theme, which is both deliberately open-ended and undecided, while typically circulating around sensitive or topical sociopolitical scenarios.

We turn, then, to *Radio Muezzin*: on the face of it a more straightforward kind of show, presented in an end-on theatre format (see Hamilton [2015], for helpful close description of elements of the performance).[3] Stefan Kaegi, who conceived and directed the production, apparently had the idea for it after

Cargo Sofia had toured to Damascus, with its overlapping calls to prayer, and Amman, where the call to prayer was broadcast (see Anon. 2009). When Kaegi made the show in 2008, there were around 30,000 mosques in Cairo. The muezzins – the men who issue the call to prayer – were usually employed by the Ministry for Religious Affairs and normally worked as caretakers to the mosques in which they served. *Radio Muezzin* featured four muezzins from Cairo, in the wake of a contentious decision by the Egyptian government to centralize the call by way of electronic broadcast. As Khalid Amine explains:

> The main objective behind this decision, according to [Mahmoud Hamdi] Zaqzouq [at the time, the Egyptian Minister of Religious Endowments], is the elimination of the "cacophony of overlapping *adhans* [calls to public prayer] and microphone wars" between neighboring *muadhinin* [muezzin], which violate the sacredness of such a ritual practice. The call will be transmitted from the mosque of al-azhar to all other official and semi-official mosques of Cairo and its neighboring areas.
>
> (Amine 2009)

The show initially focuses on three of the men who, at the time of the production, were about to give up voicing the call to prayer. Each presents himself in and through his own biographical detail. Hussein Gouda Hussein Bdawy, who is blind, lives in the suburbs of Cairo and has a two-hour journey to the mosque where he works. Abdelmoty Abdelsamia Ali Hindawy is an electrician by trade. Injured in a road accident, so that he has a number of pins in his left leg, he covers for the Imam at his mosque, giving the call to prayer on an occasional basis. Mansour Abdelsalam Mansour Namous issues the call to prayer, and to make ends meet also works the night shift in a bakery. Bdawy and Namous are employed by the Ministry of Religious Endowment, and Hindawy works in the mosque on an unofficial basis.

FIGURE 5 *Three muezzins – (left to right) Hussein Gouda Hussein Bdawy, Abdelmoty Abdelsamia Ali Hindawy and Mansour Abdelsalam Mansour Namous – at their stations in* Radio Muezzin, *directed by Stefan Kaegi, presented by Rimini Protokoll. Photo © Barbara Braun.*

In Mohamed Shoukry's design, each of the men inhabits a 'station' equidistant from each other across the rear of the stage. Each station comprises a chair and (for three of the four muezzin – we shall come to the fourth) a small table. A separate video image plays behind each when they are speaking, so that sometimes you watch just a single image associated with one of the men, or four images showing different things, or a single wide shot (often, for example, a travelling shot through the streets of Cairo) that plays across all four screens. A red carpet with a repeating geometrical pattern covers the stage. Amine observes that the production aesthetic presents a combination of collage and minimalism, with deliberate arrangements that are both formal and referential. For example, 'The red carpet with its demarcating lines is a strong indication of the inside of the mosque as a ritual space that is now transformed into a performance space' (Amine 2009).

The projections (in the video design by Bruno Deville and Shady George Fakhry) include footage of the respective mosques and images of prayer that takes place in the street. The men respectively describe their lives and their workplaces (the mosques in which they give the call to prayer), and the video echoes with images from their domestic circumstances and photos of their families and from significant events in their lives. Hindawy, for example, describes how the Imam at the mosque at which he worshipped suggested one day that he read the Qu'ran in the mosque, and then suggested he give the call to prayer – a significant responsibility – at which people praised his voice (*Radio Muezzin* 2009: 12'30 [the timecode refers to the video of the production on the company's website]).

The show includes vignettes of preparation, prayer and tasks of various kinds. The muezzins demonstrate the form of ritual and practice concerning prayer, for example, including preparatory ablutions, accompanied by an explanatory text across the rear screen: 'Ablution. Hands. Mouth. Nose. Face. Arms to the elbows. Head and ears. Feet' (17'10). This is accompanied by video images of a locker room, a sink and the sound of water. 'We already performed the evening prayer an hour ago', says one of the men. 'This is why we will not really pray now but only show the form of the prayer' (18'50). Namous makes tea at his table. He hoovers the carpet (one of his jobs in his mosque) (27'30). Hindawy also makes tea and at one point (as an electrician, perhaps) turns on three ceiling fans suspended over the stage from a console on his desk. The men perform these ubiquitous, small-scale activities as various prayer times (for example in Alexandria, Berlin and Constantinople) are indicated on the screen.

The show presents the minutiae of lived lives and humdrum quotidian detail, set amid the structuring rhythm of five times prescribed for prayer throughout the day – in a reflex that might be anti-othering, or might be a sentimental gesture to a universalist Islamic affiliation, it is always prayer-time somewhere. The muezzin re-present daily actions that have the appearance of ritual, and ritualized religious actions such as the call to prayer itself, as daily practice. In both instances, we are in the presence of a routine, something that is performed by a body (and indeed voice), to a specific pattern of action and a repeatable duration. This is one area in which observable, documentable practices become platformed by theatre – made both substantial and representative, whilst also being ephemeral. The staged routines provide a texture of lived and repeated activity that intersects with the show's socio-political reference, to do with technological adaptation, economic dependency and the integration of faith-based practices into the weft of a culture's expression of itself.

Partway through, the muezzins are joined by Sayed Abdellatif Mohamed Hammad, who introduces himself as a radio technician. His station, a desk with technical equipment, faces into the stage from close to the stage-right wing (39'40). Hammad sets up and demonstrates a transmitter that he made himself. 'In the future this technology will be used for the azan,' he says (39'40). He demonstrates how every radio within 50 metres can receive and play his voice. This piece of explanation is pedagogic. It also invites you to muse upon the implications (technologically; culturally) in this shift to centralized broadcast.

A fourth muezzin, Mohamed Ali Mahmoud Farag, is introduced around two thirds through the show (although he has been sitting at his station prior to this). He is one of the thirty selected by the ministry to perform the call to prayer in future. Unlike his colleagues, he wears a Western suit. As Hamilton observes, 'he [Farag] lives in the 6th of October City, Cairo's main satellite city ... [he is] the son of a famous Qur'an reader, and this has ensured that among his family's acquaintances are football players and politicians ... [he] holds a diploma in Islamic Studies' (2015: 83). There is, then, a form of social distinction between the men. By 2012 Farag had left the production and his lines were spoken by the assistant director, so that he was represented but not 'played' as a character. According to Kaegi, 'in a performance that is all about disappearing, about substituting people by machines or recorders or by live transmissions ... it completely made sense ... that he could be absent but his voice could still be there' (cited in Hamilton 2015: 86–7).

Whether present or not, the distinction between three men about to lose their role and one about to assume it as a state-sanctioned broadcaster, means that a dramatic irony hangs over the production. It presents the specific detail of the lives of 'ordinary' people. And yet the men are already structured by way of their differences and cannot be melded into a single representative of the Egyptian muezzin. Nor are they 'ordinary' in the face of the predominantly Western audiences to whom they performed. On the one hand, they are part of a familiar post-industrial context in which newly technologized practices leave in their wake those who are made redundant. The shift in practice regarding the call to prayer, specific to an Islamic community in the Egyptian capital, stands in for so many other socio-cultural developments that change employment practices and affect lives. On the other hand, Kaegi also presents an encounter with a culture often othered and even demonized in the West. For audiences in Helsinki, Lisbon, Sydney, or the other cities where the show was presented, this is an engagement with people whose customs, domestic circumstances and cultural practices may well be unfamiliar.

This very matter of opening access to the 'other' proved one of celebration for some and concern for others. Lyn Gardner, for example, writes in a review in the *Guardian*: 'Not only does Radio Muezzin give you a direct conduit into other people's lives and another culture, this low-key piece also grapples with the very form of theatre itself – in particular, the issues of co-authorship, ownership and exploitation that arise in documentary theatre' (Gardner 2009). The very business of representing the lives of others is also one that opens out questions of theatrical representation. For Margaret Hamilton, 'In what is arguably a laboratory for cultural negotiation, Kaegi's muezzins, at once subject and object of narration, acknowledge and disrupt not simply the fictional principles of drama, but the postdramatic theatrical frame, its de-dramatized *reality*' (Hamilton 2015: 86; original emphasis). Representation, then, is not innocent. It operates within a system of looking; and a power dynamic between those on the stage and those organizing the stage, and those on the stage and those watching it. All the more pertinent, when the subjects/objects of the piece – the Islamic others – come under the jurisdiction of a white Western European director and the gaze of predominantly white Western spectators.

This was certainly an issue for Hassan Khan, who reviewed a work-in-progress presentation of the show on 5 December 2008 at the El Sawy Culturewheel in Cairo. Khan criticizes what he saw as 'an almost infantile interest in signifiers of otherness – beards, uniforms, interiors of mosques ... [that] remained merely ethnographic and thus fetishized'. He takes particular exception to the depiction of prayer, an act whose performance – and cultural and sociopolitical ramifications – is at the centre of the production: 'we, the audience, find ourselves in the space of voyeurism, colonial history, and its contemporary descendant: tourism. The parallel to the tourist experience, where a tour group is treated to tribal dances, is inescapable'. Khan argues that this is 'a form of (in a term coined by a smart and secretly angry friend) "poornography." The privileged audience gets a taste of its unknowable nemesis, demystifying the enigma while paradoxically enhancing its mystique – a night out with a shot of feel-good humanism' (Khan 2009).

Kaegi speaks of wanting to examine both the specific circumstances of the men and the less tangible loss of prestige that would result from losing their role in the call to prayer (see for example, Anon. 2009), and it is easy to see that any such examination on the part of a Western company would inevitably find it difficult to escape structures of fetishization. That said, it is also easy to see why a company that wishes to shine a light on neoliberal practices in its own patch would be interested in not dissimilar manifestations elsewhere, not least the associated processes of technologization, rationalization and the dovetailing of centralization and decentring. In his own nuanced review of the show, Khalid Amine observes that 'In the performance, the *muadhinin* performers themselves become the text to be read' (Amine 2009). And yet, what agency do they have over the reading? In a footnote, Amine writes about an interview he and Ramona Moss undertook with the five muezzin before the performance on 5 March 2009, in which they were 'very critical' of changes to the show that Kaegi had made in Berlin.

> They insisted that the work started as a collaborative process when they were selected by Kaegi, but at the end of the interview ... they expressed a deep concern about some of the images that were projected on the screen without their consent ... They clearly wanted to make sure that their main task is preaching and that they have nothing to do with any political agendas behind the production.
> (Amine 2009: note 1)

In the event, the show was presented in a number of countries between 2009 and 2012, so the muezzin presumably found that their concerns were not terminal, perhaps in the light of the positive critical reception that the show received, and the sense that it both gave access to and respected the practices that its performers demonstrated. Nonetheless, the comments of Khan and Amine, writing from outside the subject position of the mainly Western reviewers of the piece, opens a fissure into the work of representation. Documentary theatre is nuanced here in order to stage both an instance of socio-cultural process (the change to the call to prayer, in a society negotiating the relationship between secular and religious determinants); and a figuring of the place of performance – its capacity to organize, demonstrate and complicate. Its own act of complication was itself found to be problematic.

One final reflection before we leave this piece. In securing permissions from the Ministry of Religious Endowments in Egypt to stage the piece, the company was asked to observe various constraints. In a typically reflexive and allusive move, these are projected as a scrolling text across the screen while Bdawy sings a religious song. The text includes the instructions: 'On the screens there should be no donkeys or dogs. And also no garbage or actors' (*Radio Muezzin* 2009: 52'). The latter, at least, was easy – and in relation to the stage as well as the screen. One of the key features of Rimini Protokoll's work over the years has been its involvement of so-called 'experts of the everyday' – members of the public, individuals from specific professions, people who are not professional theatre actors. As Jens Roselt has suggested, they can be seen as 'function holders' rather than characters (see Birgfeld et al 2015: xv). Their function varies across the productions. They might represent a specific area of expertise ('everyday' only insofar as it is their job or their hobby); and they provide detail about their own work or circumstances in a way that illuminates or begs questions of wider social arrangements and habits. As Birgfeld et al. suggest, 'Rimini Protokoll's performers bring with them a wealth of experiences and perspectives that throw light in particular on the reality of living in a world marked by late capitalism, mediatization and global mobility' (2015: x).

The participants in the staging might also stand in for the public, or are sometimes involved precisely as members of the public; and at that point the spectators themselves become the players. This shift from the engagement of 'experts of the everyday' taking the place of actors, to the involvement of audience members is exemplified by *100% City* – in which members of the public are gathered precisely as a group large enough to undertake survey work that has the appearance of diversity and a representational function; and *Situation Rooms*. The latter focuses on the accounts of interviewees (all of whom had a personal relation to warfare in some way) that are encountered by spectators who are themselves immersed in a game-like promenade scenario, moving through different rooms that evoke various settings and scenes. The company is not alone in this shift. In the UK, for example, the performance and media company Blast Theory has for a while been making shows without actors, where the audience member is a participant/player within game-like narratives and set-ups. And the immersive theatre scene, exemplified by Punchdrunk, involves spectators as co-participants moving through and sometimes interacting with scenic space (also, in Punchdrunk's case, with co-present actors). Given that we started this volume with Piscator's *In Spite of Everything!*, it seems only right to mention Brecht's observation that:

> Piscator was even ready to do wholly without actors. When the former German Emperor had his lawyers protest at Piscator's plan to let an actor portray him on his stage, Piscator just asked if the Emperor wouldn't be willing to appear in person; he offered him a contract, so to speak.
> (Brecht 2015: 137)

In an article in *DE* magazine, Till Briegleb raises an interesting nuance concerning the adequacy or otherwise of non-actors in a theatre setting. Actors, Briegleb suggests, are normally in the business of presenting convincing portrayals of personae drawn from the world. However:

> If the models try to represent themselves, their performance often seems unrealistic, for in the theatre the experts in real life are actually lay-people [that is, they are precisely non-professional when it comes to the business of appearing onstage] ... Although Rimini Protokoll deliberately include the embarrassment of lay theatre, as it exposes the false appearance of acted out reality theatres, the collective and their courageous actors nevertheless succeed in composing diversified sequences of scenes dealing dramatically with real themes.
> (Briegleb 2015: 50)

Briegleb articulates the complicated relationship between representation and topoi in Rimini Protokoll's work. This particular theatre practice divests performers from the role of representation – they do not play other people, but rather appear as themselves. In so doing, they draw attention precisely to the jeopardy of theatrical representation, since they cannot appear adequately as themselves (for they are in a staged construction rather than an authentic scene of labour, say, or domestic living), and always also appear precisely as vehicles of meaning-making. The deep function of the actor – to participate in staged presentation that conveys meaning – is therefore transacted in a modally different way by the experts of the everyday in Rimini Protokoll shows. In that sense, the work isn't so different from the theatre that it supplants. There remains a transaction with meaning and topic: albeit that woven into the topic is a reality effect, that is also a gesture of authentication, deriving from the use of non-actors. This returns us to the scene of documentary theatre in the twenty-first century.

Stefan Kaegi worked as a journalist before taking up the full-time occupation of theatre-maker. We turn next to the work of a journalist who, in effect, stages journalism in a Venn-diagram-like overlap of documentary enquiry and series-based entertainment.

Serial

Stefan Kaegi has suggested that Rimini Protokoll's work is 'closer to a form of journalism' (see Hamilton 2015: 73). Moving closer still, we turn next to a podcast produced by the radio programme *This American Life* – to examine more closely the meeting point between reportage, mediated presentation and cultural transaction.

Serial (2014–18) is a podcast by Sarah Koenig, an American investigative journalist, produced for the radio programme *This American Life*, a weekly public radio programme and podcast, with each programme addressing a particular theme.[4] *Serial* (series 1) was the first podcast to be downloaded over a million times, the fastest to reach 5 million downloads on iTunes and (according to *Variety*) has been downloaded over 340 million times. The first series, released in 2014, considered the case of Adnan Syed, serving a life sentence for the murder of his girlfriend in 1999. Koenig narrates an investigative account that considers a range of testimonies, some of them sourced from trial proceedings and some from interviews conducted by the presenter, to explore anomalies and contradictions in the case. My focus here is Koenig's second series, aired in 2015–16.[5] This explores the case of American soldier Bowe Bergdahl, who was held by the Taliban for five years before being released in a prisoner exchange, whereupon he was brought before a court martial on grounds of desertion and subsequently dishonourably discharged.

One of the areas of discussion for reviewers and aficionados of the series concerned distinctions between Series 1 and 2. The first series was a runaway success: as the blurb on the *New York Times* website indicates, 'When it launched in 2014, "Serial" became a global sensation that has been credited with launching

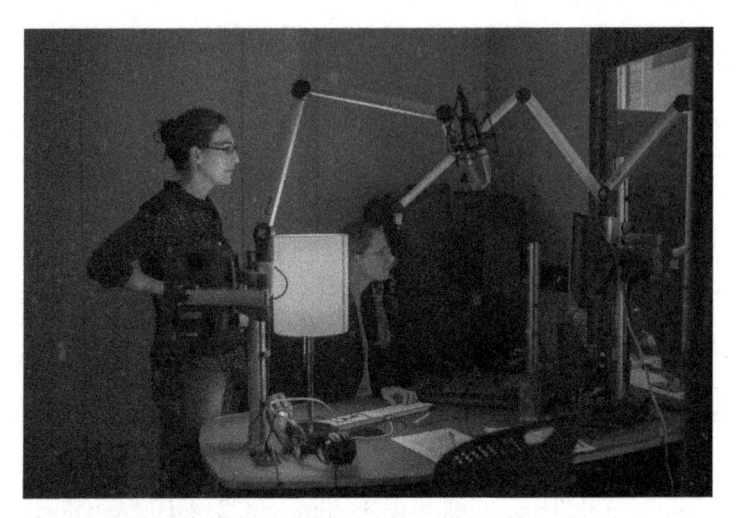

FIGURE 6 *Sarah Koenig (left) and producer Dana Chivvis in the studio during the making of* Serial. *Photo: Elise Bergerson.*

the modern era of audio journalism' (Serial Productions 2022). (Perhaps the *NYT* would run this, as it acquired Serial Productions in 2020.) However, the listener figures for Season 2 initially seemed considerably smaller than those for Season 1. Melissa Locker in the *Guardian* puts what the paper headlines as a 'slump' down to a mix of over-complexity and under-dramatization. Nonetheless, she acknowledges that 'Serial was always meant to be experimental, starting with its serialized format, and it seems clear that season two was another attempt to try something new in podcasting – very, very long form reporting of a complicated case' (Locker 2016). Chris Nashawaty reports that 'Koenig and executive producer Julie Snyder said the download numbers for season 2 (50 million) were higher than they were by the time season 1 ended its run' (Nashawaty 2016) – and Nashawaty's summary reverberates the notion of this as an ambitiously complex piece: 'it was a season that defied most of our conventional expectations of narrative. It wasn't a story with a beginning, middle, and, most importantly, an end' (2016).

This is partly due to the peculiar circumstance of the case. Berghdal was a private in the US army. He had previously been stood down from coastguard training on account of mental health difficulties. The army had recruited him during a relaxation in recruitment protocols given a surge in deployment to Iran and Afghanistan. Bergdahl had been posted to Afghanistan. By his account, he witnessed and was on the wrong end of what he described as inappropriate decision-making and leadership on the part of his platoon commanders. He contrived to leave his camp and, at some point shortly thereafter, was picked up by the Taliban. By Bergdahl's account, he had left in order to walk to a different base – around 24 hours away – and in so doing draw attention to the poor leadership in his own facility. And yet, this plan seemed barely feasible. Bergdahl comes over as something of a romantic and an idealist, but stories subsequently circulated of him as a Taliban sympathizer. In the event, Bergdahl remained in captivity – other than for a couple of short-lived escape attempts – for five years. Initially search parties were deployed, but it seems that Bergdahl was moved quite quickly to Pakistan, where it was easier for the Taliban to conceal him. Eventually he was released as part of a prisoner exchange, with the United States swapping five prisoners who had been held in the facility at Guantanamo Bay. The exchange itself was controversial in the United States. The Obama administration had to skirt protocol and not seek Defense Department clearance for the trade, in order to keep it secret until the last minute. President Obama gave a probably ill-advised public address in the Rose Garden of the White House, flanked by Bergdahl's parents. And the next day Susan Rice, White House National Security Advisor, said during an interview that Bergdahl had behaved with 'honour and distinction'. This proved too much for members of his platoon, for whom he was a maverick who had put his colleagues in danger and betrayed his country.

Zach Baron gives the positive case for Series 2:

> the second season of *Serial* has been astonishingly good, albeit in a more sprawling kind of way than season one ... [It] was an invaluable document of what it was like to serve in the modern, often purposeless wars we've been fighting since 9/11 ... And the way Bergdahl's story grew and knotted to include President Obama and Guantanamo and unofficial geopolitical negotiations in Europe and two random intel analysts in Florida? *Serial* grew and knotted to encompass it all, too.
>
> (Baron 2016)

This long-form, complicated, multifarious kind of journalism is a particular kind of extension of the documentary drive of the 1990s and early 2000s. It seeks to uncover facts and explain events, drawing on testimony – and it does so by organizing its material broadly around a narrative arc (albeit that, as Locker says, 'This season had no cliffhangers' [2016]) – in this instance, the timeline of Bergdahl's disappearance, capture, incarceration and return. Across this arc, the various episodes are arranged more thematically, dealing with the efforts of Bergdahl's friends in the United States to locate him or demand that US agencies locate him; the experience of soldiers who went looking for him; and reflections upon Bergdahl's treatment while in captivity, his psychological state and how he managed to sustain himself. In her Season 2 Welcome podcast, Koenig writes:

> This story—it spins out in so many unexpected directions … It reaches into swaths of the military, the peace talks to end the war, attempts to rescue other hostages, our Guantanamo policy. What Bergdahl did made me wrestle with things I'd thought I more or less understood, but really didn't: what it means to be loyal, to be resilient, to be used, to be punished.[6]

Koenig articulates a nexus of questions and reverberations that are similar to those accompanying the verbatim and tribunal work that we considered in Chapter 3. *Serial* removes the 'staging' of civic proceedings. Instead, it presents instances, testimonies and available evidence in a way that packages the case both as a series-format entertainment output and a long-form investigative enquiry that seeks to uncover the facts of the matter. Let's consider some excerpts, the first from the start of Episode 2. Koenig says:

> The army's decision to go to court-martial – its not that it's so surprising. I mean, this was always a strong possibility. It's just, for a lot of people watching Bowe's case, it's been hard to handicap. All outward signs have pointed to an army that is of two minds about how to deal with what Bowe did – whether to throw the book at him, or whether to say, OK, yes, he screwed up in a huge way, but five years with the Taliban, enough is enough.
>
> (*Serial* 2.2: 2'00)[7]

Koenig observes how it seems that individual senior figures in the military establishment are ready to forgive Bergdahl, while the army as an institution wants to prosecute him (noting that desertion carries the possibility of a prison sentence, possibly for life).

The excerpt is a good example of Koenig working through the competing positions, sifting the material, and speaking directly to the listener in a structured but informal register – a direct seam, here, of the pedagogic principle of the documentary, with the more situated individual engagement of the reporter in an auto-ethnographic journey of discovery. Towards the end of this episode, Koenig interviews soldiers from Bergdahl's platoon:

> Daryl Hansen: If we would've found him, I think a lot of us would have shot him if that tells you anything.
> Sarah Koenig: That's Daryl Hansen, one of Bowe's platoon mates.
> Daryl Hansen: I truly say that with sincerity, that we had that much hate towards him.
> ...
> Sarah Koenig: I found this shocking, and disturbing, that some of these guys were saying they might have killed Bowe if they'd found him, but now after interviewing more than a dozen soldiers, I still don't sympathise with wanting to kill him, but I do understand why their anger was so extreme, I get it.
>
> (*Serial* 2.2: 30'19)

Koenig moves quickly and easily between direct address to the listener and interviews with soldiers and other participants. Bergdahl's presence in the tapes is both as witness but also as mystery presence, someone around whose person reverberates various mysteries and challenges. Koenig provides the thread for the listener; as an 'everywoman' asking questions that are both obvious and sequential, but also as a journalist posing questions to players in the story. She filters and layers testimony, interview, media intervention and interpretation. In so doing, she performs a navigation of public interest and professional agency that is part of the wider fusion of personal/individual and public/shared that has become ubiquitous in twenty-first-century communications culture, not least through the proliferation of rolling news coverage, the suffusion of actuality and entertainment programming, and the extension of social media to enable real-time reportage and personalized commentary.

In Episode 11 Koenig addresses the key question as to whether soldiers in Bergdahl's regiment were killed looking for him. She notes that amid a plethora of stories in the media on this topic, there are normally six soldiers from Bergdahl's battalion who are repeatedly named. She acknowledges that 'there was a massive search for Bowe' over the month following his departure from the base; 'But, rather miraculously, no one died on those missions. The six names of soldiers who died, they were all on missions that happened later' (*Serial* 2.11: 9'22).

Writing in *IndieWire* in 2018, just before the launch of *Series* Season 3, Steve Green recalls a spicy exchange in Season 2 between Koenig and Lieutenant General Michael Flynn, who argued that Bergdahl must have caused the deaths of American soldiers who were despatched to search for him (the same Michael Flynn who would become the US National Security Advisor for the first three weeks of Donald Trump's administration). As Green drily suggests, '"Serial" Season 2 now exists in a far more different context than when it was first produced' (Greene 2018).

After the series ended, Koenig wrote a follow-up post on 10 June 2016, under the headline 'Was Anyone Killed Looking for Bowe Bergdahl? Some Hard Evidence, at Long Last.' She notes the release of the US Army's internal investigation into the deaths of the six soldiers from Bergdahl's unit. 'Here's what we've learned: None of these investigations report that any of these men was on a mission to look for Bergdahl. Neither Bergdahl's name, nor the term DUSTWUN (shorthand for a missing soldier), appears in any of the documents' (Koenig 2016).

Let's end with Koenig's interview with Lieutenant Colonel Paul Edgar, who managed the search for Bergdahl. Edgar reflects on whether Bergdahl was an anomaly, or – perhaps counter-intuitively – simply a part of the ecosystem of a deployment in hostile territory. He observes that following the hijackings and suicide attacks carried out on US targets by al-Qaida on 11 September 2001, there was an acceptance of military action in Afghanistan and other territories – but without proper acknowledgement of the various mistakes and consequences (including the rush to recruitment) that is all part of the effort.

> Sarah Koenig: Paul said we signed up for Afghanistan ... But when we signed up, we were also signing up for all the things we tend to forget but that nevertheless attend war ...
> Paul Edgar: So there's a level of responsibility here, whether it's, whether it's Bowe and his particulars, or the things, the baggage of war that goes along with every single one, that we signed up for as a society. And to take all of that, and to pin it, politically and otherwise, uh, on um, you know, this twenty-year-old, er, is in my opinion, erm, very very wrong.
> (*Serial* 2.11: 51:10)

Why have I chosen to discuss an investigative radio series in a book about documentary theatre? *Serial* inhabits an expanded landscape of theatres of the real. It enacts 'writing' as a multi-part activity, weaving testimony from interviews, reportage and personal reflection. It moves across very intimate and individual experience, not least those of Bergdahl in confinement; and highly public, geopolitical concerns with regard to the US presence in Afghanistan and the army's protocols in looking after its own (in whatever context that might be and however one might define it). It situates the journalist at the heart of the enquiry – it is both objective in its search for the facts that are 'out there', and subjective in that Koenig's presence and reactions keep this grounded as the enquiry of an individual (who also represents a larger production team). In this mix of subject and object we recall Rimini Protokoll's muezzin. Their function is to share aspects of their own life rather than look into the lives of others, but there is nonetheless an overlap in both productions between rhetorical objectivity and situated individual experience. *Serial* manages its material right at the interface of reportage and entertainment. It unpacked the details of a story that accumulated in complexity, operating around tropes of narrative (what happened next?), character (what kind of person was this?) and consequence (how widely does this reach?). It presented material unearthed through journalistic research and interviews with key figures, whilst it rewarded the ongoing engagement of its audience through the series format, packaging themes within its respective episodes while developing the long-form storyline. As observed previously, this was nonetheless a story without enticing cliffhangers or even a satisfactory ending. Yet this was a further indicator of the programme's reality effect, and thereby the pleasure it offers of a dramaturgically constructed engagement with questions concerning actuality – in a miasma of individual experience (separately, both Bergdahl's and Koenig's), amid the massive churn of military protocol, national (US) identity and geopolitics.

Each week the production team posted 'assets' on the show's website – maps; artwork concerning aspects of the story; videos including those released by the Taliban as proof that Bergdahl was alive and in captivity; photos; org charts – a plethora of resources that extended the podcast as an accumulation of reference points. This ever-expanding referentiality, indeed the programme's entire discursive arrangement, circulates around – and never conclusively arrives at – the truth of the matter. As Steve Greene suggests,

> "Serial" became a precursor to a mammoth shift in public attitudes to what can and can't be constituted as absolute truth … The value of "Serial" isn't in the length of the investigation, it's in the volume of perspective … the show has an admirable meticulous devotion to context.
>
> (Greene 2018)

It is this devotion that in part addresses the anxiety around the ever-escaping categories of truth, actualization and authentication. We turn next to a piece that stages this crisis of truth as a deliberate artistic strategy that *de-reals* the practices of documenting and recording, by simultaneously staging the work of making real.

The House of European History in Exile

Thomas Bellinck is a Belgian theatre-maker with a long track record in developing documentary-oriented work, across various media. In 2010 he co-founded the theatre company Steigeisen, focusing on producing documentary plays. In 2015 he co-founded ROBIN, described on the company's website as 'a Brussels-based production structure supporting socially engaged art practices ... As a collectively autonomous society of artists working in and across multiple disciplines, ROBIN embraces a made-to-measure artistic productional approach'.[8]

At KASK/HoGent (The Royal Academy of Fine Arts (KASK) and the Royal Conservatory constitute the school of arts of HOGENT and Howest) Bellinck co-founded the School of Speculative Documentary, which I understand to be rather more of a gesture (and an academic module with summative symposium) than a separate institution with an ongoing programme of study. Here's some of the introductory blurb from the outline for a course unit entitled 'The School of Speculative Documentary – "If the Heart Could Think it Would Stop Beating"', offered in the Academic Year 2018–19:

> The School of Speculative Documentary is ... a cross-disciplinary meeting place dedicated to critically questioning the documentary gesture. The artists associated

with the School of Speculative Documentary openly embrace uncertainty, messiness and conjecture in their engagement with and creation of multiple and mutable realities ... How can we rethink the documentary gesture conceptually, formally and methodologically, exposing it to continuous uncertainty, contamination and contestation?[9]

Bellinck had already proposed an answer to these questions in the project that we focus on next. He developed *Domo de Eŭropa Historio en Ekzilo* (which translates from the tactically selected Esperanto as *The House of European History in Exile*) in 2013, and after opening in Brussels the project was presented in Rotterdam, Vienna, Athens, Wiesbaden and Marseille at various points through to 2018.[10] Bellinck describes the work as a 'speculative documentary' by way of a museum from the future, commemorating a time (the beginning of the twenty-first century) when the European Union still existed. Influenced by Agamben's idea of the 'apparatus', Bellinck talks of 'a documentary gesture that openly embraces uncertainty and bases itself on conjecture rather than knowledge' (Bellinck 2018: Video 7: 0.05). Drawing on Foucault's idea of the dispositive, Agamben conceives the apparatus as a set of networks, relationships, institutions and discourses that contain and entrap the very people who created it. *The House of European History in Exile* thus purports to unmask and unfix both the apparatus that is the European Union, and the differently organizational apparatus that is the museum as a settled repository of historical evidence and latter-day knowledge. The project is described in its marketing information as a 'performance-installation' and an 'immersive experience'.[11] It arranges materials for spectating and situates the spectator within the piece. It allows us to address an entropic or exhausted or baroque documentary situation – where we witness all the appearance of the document as it simultaneously declares its own fakery, fiction and parody.

On 25 October 2018 Bellinck gave a keynote lecture about his work at the inaugural EASTAP (European Association for

FIGURE 7 *An installation within* Domo de Eŭropa Historio en Ekzilo (The House of European History in Exile), *conceived and realized by Thomas Bellinck, Festival de Marseille Mucem, Fort Saint-Jean (2013). Photo: Danny Willems.*

the Study of Theatre and Performance) conference in Paris. He describes the project as the deployment of documentary strategies in service of 'what if rather than the mimetic as if'; and, given the futuristic setting of the work, the depiction of 'pre-enactments rather than re-enactments' (Bellinck 2018: Video 3: 2.55). Spectators enter the installation one by one, with five minutes between each entry so that, as Bellinck says, 'you are completely on your own in this cruddy, dusty, abandoned museum' (2018: Video 6). There is no natural daylight, and a deliberately labyrinthine set-up. Exhibits have a clapped-out and even nonsensical aspect. For example, a leek overlays a framed formal-looking directive. Translucent plastic sheeting covers a photograph of delegates at table, microphones before them, or the wooden doors that appear to be the entrance to a chamber (we know not what). Old office paraphernalia is jumbled together, along with official-seeming portraits and maps. Juxtapositions are ironic and allusive, including a collation of colonial artefacts alongside a collection of contemporary business cards (as you might find in the drop-bowl at the reception of a hotel). The gathering of materials is wittingly banal and unmoors the objects from their referential and contextual grounding – which, you might say, is exactly what a museum does, albeit that museum curators usually work hard to provide precisely the kind of contextualization that is missing here.

The visitor's journey through the installation ends with a letter that Bellinck has written to the father of a childhood friend who committed suicide while Bellinck was working on the project. In the EASTAP keynote, he tells how his friend, a tomato farmer, had struggled to compete with other farms using 'illegalized migrants', and in the process of innovating his own production he went bankrupt and subsequently committed suicide. The letter, Bellinck says, 'really became a huge rupture ... in how the museum functions' (2018: Video 8: 4.54) – that's to say, it was not part of the fictitious and playful register of the piece, not part of the game (perhaps, rather, it changed the nature and register of the game).

> And then after this space you end up in the bar, because every good museum has a museum bar ... I was at the bar myself, so I served drinks, and I don't tell people that I built the thing that they went through, of course, and then we discuss the exhibition, basically.
> (2018: Video 8: 5.00)

The artist is playfully present in one last ruse of slippage in full view, facilitating a final mode of engagement for the spectator (with actual conversation over an actual drink) as a palimpsestic coda to the piece, and part of a multi-textured return to reality. This is all in keeping with Bellinck's larger oeuvre, which demonstrates a pattern of concern with the nature, function and transactional processes of the museum as an institution, and the slippages between observation, representation and individual engagement.

After working on *Domo*, Bellinck collaborated with a number of artists on a project entitled *Counter-Museum of Individual Freedoms*, produced in and with L'Art Rue, an experimental arts space in Tunis. The project was conducted as a deliberately reflective response to the ten-year anniversary of the Tunisian Revolution of December 2020-January 2021, which led to the deposition of President Zine El Abidini Ben Ali, who had been in power for twenty-three years, and the establishment of elections on a democratic model. The revolution was the inaugural event in the 'Arab Spring' sequence of protests that took place over the next couple of years. The Counter-Museum is described on Bellinck's website as a 'transdisciplinary Collective process', and the reader is addressed as follows:

> Hello. Welcome. You've entered a construction site. We are a group of amateur-museologists, artists, researchers, activists and co-citizens from within and outside of Tunisia. 10 Years after the start of the Revolution, we are working here on the creation of a 'Counter-Museum of Individual Liberties' ... how to build a museum that is not some cold and silent freezer of an official past? How to build a museum that lives and breathes and moves together with the people who construct and visit it.[12]

Bellinck subsequently developed *Simple as ABC*, a multi-part series of plays concerning human mobility management. The sixth in the series, for instance, entitled *The Museum of Human-Hunting*, is an audio piece presented as part of the *Radically Naive/Naively Radical* exhibition in Antwerp, 5–11 July 2021. It features re-enactments of three interviews that Bellinck conducted with European Union 'border managers' working for the European Union, which (as the website blurb has it) 'promotes international freedom of movement for some, while making it illegal for others'.[13]

Here is a body of work, then, that undertakes a documentary-style presentation of materials, including testimonies, objects, texts and artefacts, while asking the spectator to adjudicate – and take pleasure in – the unstable and ephemeral nature of the relationship between document (material) and referent. This returns us to D'Ancona's concern that in a post-postmodern, post-truth environment, stable and shared reference points have been relativized and emptied out. The artist, in Bellinck's case, draws our attention to this rather than seeks to recuperate a stable meaning amid the churn of representational flux and uncertainty. The shift – and it is the same as that which D'Ancona outlines as a characteristic of a post-truth political culture – is from an agreement concerning shared facts to an engagement through individual experience. Bellinck manages this through the organization of the journey of visitor-spectators, and subsequently the engagement of artists and participants in the project of co-creating a 'counter-museum' whose reality exists in transactional exchanges between participating individuals around matters of value. We have moved, then, from facts to values and from common agreements to individual expressions of identity and affiliation.

The Wall

My next instance centres on the specific situation of individuals who appear online to the audience (gathered in the theatre). When I saw the show it suffered considerably from internet connection difficulties, so I focus here rather more on the concept than the performance outcome. *The Wall*, directed by Juan Ayala and presented in Madrid and Bristol by Teatro de la Abadía and Tobacco Factory Theatres (2023) stages a set of live encounters: one between two performers in different continents who (for geopolitical reasons) are unable to travel and appear online, on a large screen at the back of the stage; and between co-present performers on the stage, who help facilitate

FIGURE 8 El Muro (The Wall), *presented by Teatro de La Abadía and Tobacco Factory Theatres. The image is from the version of the production presented at Sala José Luis Alonso, Madrid, 2023. On screen (left to right): Igor Shugaleev, Mokhallad Rasem. On stage (left to right): Freddy Wiegand, Maite Jáuregui, Chumo Mata, Ksenia Guinea. Photo © Juan Millás.*

and interpret their encounter – thereby providing a refracted encounter with the audience.[14]

The performers online appear as themselves, introduce themselves and ask each other questions. The performance that I saw featured two theatre workers (a slight finesse of Claire Bishop's 'delegated performance', perhaps, as discussed in Chapter 1 – here the non-actors are specialists in theatre). Mohdad left Baghdad ten years ago. His home is in Belgium. He is eating dates. He is a theatre director. Magda is from El Salvador. She makes theatre that addresses gender violence and other social issues.

> Mohdad: Magda, how is your daily mobility?
> Magda: We don't have constitutional rights to move around. There's always a fear of going out into the streets. There's military everywhere.

...
> Magda: Do you feel like you belong in Belgium?
> Mohdad: Erm, erm, yes, yes. Sometimes your soul and your body is in one place.
> I remember my mother gave me a scarf, and it had her scent on it. And I always wear scarves in my life.
> And you feel your mum is close to you. This is what belonging is to me – the simple things.

After the conversation has proceeded for a while, a text appears on the screen: 'This conversation will end in 1 minute' – a note to all concerned that conversations (in this production, at least), are tidily segmented.

In Chapter 1 I suggested that the twinned notion of revelation and intervention provides a significant mutual dynamic in documentary performance. What of that here? In *The Wall* the participants interview each other in real time, not so much as a formal transaction but in a mode closer to shared curiosity and a kind of gesture of naivety (I take this to arise from an assumption on the part of the performers of their task to lead the audience swiftly to the defining circumstance of the performers' lives). This makes the piece notably gentle and discursive (and arguably also sentimental), but it also personalizes the respective individual stories in the moment of their revelation. The texture is different from that of (say) a chat show format, since both participants are positioned equally in the discussion, and the underpinning premise of the project is therefore to reveal commonalities and differences in their respective situations and experiences. The arrangement of the show around real-time online presence matters here: geographical separation cut across by digital connectivity provides a key thematic trope: the Other Elsewhere is (let's say) a co-respondent here. The use of onstage performers to amplify the encounter – they act as interlocutors and provide a form of simultaneous translation – (re-)theatricalizes the production for the spectators in the auditorium. The device pulls the dialogue into the theatrical space, without diminishing the actuality of separation on which the show depends. And as Miguel Oyarzun, the show's dramaturg, said to me after the show: 'Every night is a premiere', given that each performance features a fresh conversation between different participants. Amid the larger project of cross-continental connection, then, is a reflex towards a theatrical mode of co-presence and the ephemeral one-off.

Much of the material for documentary theatre arises from interviews and witness statements. These are usually conducted in advance of the shaping of the performance – whether by the writer/director in interviews with subjects, or in civic and judicial proceedings, or preparatory work with participants in the production process. *The Wall* marks a shift from a hierarchical interview structure to an exchange that has the more demotic and interactive flavour of social media. The intervention is therefore arguably more equitable. The principle of revelation remains central.

We turn lastly in this chapter to a theatre production by five female poets of colour, who help demonstrate how that-which-is-documented also changes amid this cultural shift in theatres of the real.

Even at the Risk

In an unprepossessing street in Kreuzberg, a couple of blocks from the former location of the Berlin Wall, is the Ballhaus Naunynstrasse. Kreuzberg was once home to a large population of Ashkenazy Jews, many of whom lost their lives during the Holocaust. After the Second World War Kreuzberg located in the American sector in West Germany, an unfashionable down-at-heel district more or less in the shadow of the Wall. It is now a lively hub for small, independent shops, cafes and restaurants, noted for its large Turkish population and subcultural feel. How appropriate, then, amid this history of churn and immigration, that Kreuzberg should house one of the most notable theatre venues in Europe (if you believe that theatres should restage the culture in which they find themselves).

The Ballhaus Naunynstrasse defines itself as a 'post-migrant theatre', and as such (as indicated on its website):

> has offered an institutionalised stage, a space for protagonists with immigration experience and their stories; a new space for cultural vibrancy.
>
> Since 2013 ... Black perspectives, perspectives of Color and queer perspectives have increasingly been the focal point. Since then, this theatre has acted as a driving force for reflection on post-colonial structures in everyday life as well as in the arts, it intervenes for the social processing of Germany's colonial history, structural racism and intersectional exclusionary mechanisms.[15]

FIGURE 9 *(Left to right) Josephine Papke, TRVANIA, Ana Lucão, Melanelle B. C. Hémêfa and Lahya S. Aukongo, in a publicity shot for* Even at the Risk, *a Ballhaus Naunynstrasse production. Photo: Zé de Paiva.*

Even at the Risk presents spoken-word performance from five Black women.[16] Apart from one duologue these are individual performances. The women sit in the front row on either side of the stage and take turns to step onto the raised low platform that constitutes the performing area. A microphone on a stand is placed centre stage, and Lya Kifle sits at a drum kit in the upstage-right corner. The arrangement is simple and provides a focus on the respective performers, who present poems in German or English, sometimes reading from scripts. The texts become a cartography of identity, expressly articulating what it is to be a Black woman in this place, at this time.

In a piece entitled 'Sister', TRVANIA speaks to her siblings. 'You see, I'm lost and confused, brother ... I was born surrounded by Blackness ... both proud and ashamed ... but brother, I refuse to be a tragedy'. Ana Lucão says, 'Do not ask me where I am from. Rather where I am made of ... My body is a body to the land of my mothers, whose tongue I do not speak.' Stefanie-Lahya Aukongo performs 'A Black poem of colour':

> I was the oppressed hurricane blowing on its own atmosphere ... Here, here I am ... You cannot love me if your love is not political. You cannot love me if your soul is not in the intersectional mode ... There's no you without us. And there's no us without me.

Kifle occasionally punctuates and interacts with the spoken words on the drum kit, and at various points the performers give affirmatory clicks of their fingers in response to specific utterances by their colleague onstage. For example, when Melanelle B. C. Hémêfa says 'Our existence is resistance' there is a texture of clicking, a soft underscore of affiliation.

I have chosen to end this chapter with this piece, since it takes us back to Berlin, nearly 100 years after Piscator's *In Spite of Everything!*, and helps us to chart some distinctions between the documentary impulse then and now. Piscator presided over a multimedia play that dealt with developments in national and international politics, in which actors played historical figures along with representative members of society. In 2023 five Black women speak one by one into a microphone, directly to the audience, about their own identity. It is their individual experience that is the focus – rather than facts, dates, the actions of players in the civic sphere, or the quotidian details of everyday life. I opened this chapter by considering issues raised by Matthew D'Ancona in *Post Truth*. In his own affective assertion, D'Ancona concludes that 'More than ever, truth requires an emotional delivery system that speaks to experience, memory and hope' (2017: 130). *Even at the Risk* offers just that. It is the women's utterance that provides a spoken document of inner inscription. This is surely the case in other poetry readings and rap performances. The inclusion of this performance, here, is by way of arguing for an expansion of both the mode and the topic of documentary. The originary source is the live experience of individuals; the documentary assemblage is a form of reportage from identity. And this extension of testament and treatment brings us back to the longitudinal trajectories we considered in Chapter 1, and the changing nature of documentary in the twenty-first century.

5

Coda

Documentary theatre stages perspectives on 'the real, the actual, the raw and the true' (Schneider 2011: 16). Yet the way it does so changes, and ideas and assumptions about actuality and truth change too. If documentary is always after the real, it's also the case that, as Michael Renov proposed, 'Every documentary representation depends upon its own detour from the real' (1993: 7). As we have seen, documentary theatre and performance productions deploy aesthetic strategies and turn to the recording technologies of their day to access the real but, in the process, they make their own shaping intervention: they *de-real*, or *re-real*. The work of framing, staging, mediating and reiterating produces both a new assemblage and a necessarily selective perspective on the topic rather than a transparent copy of it.

In the introduction to their volume on documentary theatre, Forsyth and Megson argue that 'The once trenchant requirement that the documentary form should necessarily be equivalent to an unimpeachable and objective witness to public events has been challenged in order to situate historical truth as an embattled site of contestation' (2009: 3). This is one of the ways in which understanding of documentary as a project has changed. The function of documentary might still be to capture what's out there and bring it to attention, but there's a broader acknowledgement concerning the effects of the presence of the artist; and the instability of the subject of the record, the record itself and the context of its reception. Indeed, as Carol Martin suggests, 'In one sense, there is no recoverable "original event" because the archive is already an operation of power (who decides what is archived, and how?)' (2006: 10). Martin goes on to consider the work of interpretation in theatrical production: 'Ironically, then, it is precisely what is not in the archive, what is added by making the archive into repertory, that infuses documentary theatre with its particular theatrical viability' (2006: 11). 'Repertory' in this analysis, as we have seen, denotes the embodied and experiential practices of a culture. Documentary theatre draws upon this wider array of meaningful evidence, and in so doing becomes itself part of the repertoire – in both its ephemeral offer to its audiences and its lasting traces (texts, images, recordings) that help shape a response to a topic and an understanding of its significance.

Documentary theatre often performs a primary function of presentation (sharing situations and experiences that may not be well-known or familiar). There are nonetheless challenges concerning representation. Documentary always locates at an intersection between realities and imaginaries, or to put it another way, between the actual and the aesthetic. In the course of this book we've encountered the notion of 'truth' in cultural production; ever-developing technologies of mediation; and shifting perspectives on what's important to document and how the stuff that's available should be shaped and shared in scenarios of the actual. Documentary theatre is often staged at the fault lines of a culture, exposing, exploring, explaining and sometimes exhuming. As with all artistic forms, it is subject to experimentation, trend and taste. In that sense it marks developments in cultural production – from the introduction of screen-based materials in theatre in the 1920s, to the vernacular expression of community through song and drama in the 1970s, to the prevalence of eye-witness accounts in the verbatim and testimony-based theatre of the 1990s and beyond, to the conceptually ironic and de-dramatized work of 'reality trend' theatre.

Meanwhile theatre itself is amended. For example, the decision to use transcripts in verbatim form was key to documentary theatre supplanting the political drama of the 1970s and 1980s and marked a distillation of the more aesthetically mixed documentary drama of the previous generation. Plays (written by playwrights) were superseded by texts (composited by editors), and the texts were the records of actual utterance, whose reproduction onstage provided a curiously palimpsestic reality effect. In this formal texture we find the late-twentieth-century tributaries that feed and are refigured by the characteristically synergized flows of the 2000s: fixated with truth and full of irony, even cynicism; passionate about the authentic and obsessed with presentation. A common challenge to the form during this period concerns the nature of 'authorship' undertaken by the writer/editor and director, and whether their arrangements could ever be free of bias (if that were in any case desirable). This very feature – a sort of collaging of witness – was part of verbatim theatre's contribution to a dispersal of *auteurship* in favour of a proliferation of perspectives that properly took wing in the digital revolution provided by Web 2.0 technologies. Indeed, there is a refiguring of epistemology here, that's marked by the move from our case studies in Chapter 3 (the 1990s) to those of Chapter 4 (the 2010s and 2020s). The work of Anna Deavere Smith, for example, equitably visits perspectives across political divides. The tribunal plays provide a condensed account of what is already a formalized civic examination of events. Both arrange a discursive balance, whereas the work of the twenty-first century seeks to *get inside* an identity and play out the dimensions of an experience, a project that is necessarily more situated and partial, and perhaps less open to challenge concerning its evidence base (amid a culture in which common agreement is in meltdown).

Developments in the documentary form also track the political resonance of matters of perspective – *whose* story, *whose* telling, *whose* truth? In this it participates in a fluctuating historical churn concerning permission (to speak); the nature and dependability of mediation; verifiability; and appropriate response (what should we make of this/what should be done about this?). There is a larger philosophical and epistemological matter: the status of 'truth' in social transaction, and the certainty or otherwise over what is held to be 'real'. In this respect, documentary performance contributes to latter-day concerns with authenticity and actuality – but really to a much longer-running set of negotiations over 'fact' in private experience and public discourse, and realism in artistic production.

Minou Arjomand suggests that 'most contemporary documentary theatre either frames the performance as a direct expression of reality or questions how reality is framed by theatre and other media' (2018: 15). This isn't too far from the twin perspectives with which I opened this volume, which argued that the real is the object of theatre (Piscator) or that the theatre itself needs to be real (Rau). In considering the kind of theatre that he made himself, Erwin Piscator reflected: 'Were I asked to put a name to this style I would call it in the first instance Neorealist (not to be confused with the Naturalist style of the nineties)' ([1929] 1980: 121). I've argued above that the naturalist theatre of the nineteenth century laid some rather firmer foundations for documentary practitioners, but Piscator raises a useful qualification. A case can be made that most developments in documentary performance are neorealist since they typically involve harnessing contemporary techniques and media to present actuality in a striking new way. Meanwhile the quotation from Milo Rau that I cited at the top of the volume is preceded by this sentence: 'It's not just about portraying the world anymore. It's about changing it' (2018: 281). Rau writes as an avowedly political theatre director, but he articulates a presumption that runs through much documentary theatre practice, certainly across the productions covered in this volume.

The documentary form provides theatre practitioners with a profoundly well-geared mechanism for the kind of social engagement that is immediate, urgent and vivid. If documentary is a transposition (from another time and place, circumstance, experience), it achieves its effects in the present tense of both its making and its reception. And this brings us back to the compelling negotiation between a spectator and a situation, geared around actualities. This is endlessly involving – for if the truth is out there, it needs a lot of sifting.

NOTES

Chapter 1

1. For an exemplary collection of programmes, see https://www.bbc.co.uk/iplayer/group/p03szck8 (accessed 18 August 2023).
2. Schneider discusses time and temporality in performance more fully in her chapter 'In the Meantime: Performance Remains' (2011: 87–110; see also Wickstrom 2018).
3. Blythe discusses her work in Hammond and Steward (2008: 79–102).
4. See Rebellato (2010) for a discussion of some of the contradictions in and responses to Zola's project, and for discussion of 'two main strands' to naturalism, 'the sociological imagination' and a 'visual culture' (9–13). Note also, as Paget points out, that naturalism can in effect pickle the past and foreclose the kind of 'interruption' that documentary theatre prioritizes (2009: 224–9); we should be mindful of the distinctions between naturalism as a toolbox to replicate the real and as an artistic procedure that occludes contemporary realities.
5. *The Mandalorian* (season 1) 2019, [streaming TV series] USA: Disney+. See, for example, 'The Virtual Production of *The Mandalorian*, Season 1', in the webpage 'What is extended reality (XR)?', Mo-Sys Academy, 26 October 2020, https://www.mo-sys.com/what-is-extended-reality/ (accessed 13 August 2023).
6. *The Drowned Man* (2013), dir. Felix Barratt and Maxine Doyle, presented by Punchdrunk in collaboration with the Royal National Theatre, Temple Studios, London.
7. *Nanook of the North* (1922) [film] dir. Robert Flaherty, US: Pathé Exchange. Available online: https://www.youtube.com/watch?v=lkW14Lu1IBo (accessed 13 August 2023).

8 *Man with a Movie Camera* (1929) [Film], dir. Dziga Vertov, Soviet Union: All Ukrainian Photo Cinema Administration (VUFKU). Available online: BFI Player, https://www.youtube.com/watch?v=cGYZ5847FiI (accessed 13 August 2023).

9 In this volume I focus on productions and scholarship predominantly in a European and North American context. For discussions of late-twentieth- and twenty-first-century documentary theatre in other parts of the world, see, for instance, Hernández (2021, Latin America), Hutchison (2010, South Africa), Peters (2017, Australia), and Sowinśka (2010, Poland). For an edition in French of readings and essays, see Magris and Picon-Vallin (2019).

10 Youker tracks documentary tendencies over a longer period than I cover in this volume; and considers an array of work from the plays of Georg Büchner in the early nineteenth century to the work of Handspring Puppet Theatre (see Youker 2018).

11 See Paget (1990: 70–3) on the Stoke documentary method – foregrounding factual source material, extensive use of music and the vocabulary of 'new media', particularly radio.

12 See http://www.massobs.org.uk/ (accessed 15 August 2023).

13 Norton-Taylor and, separately, Kent, discuss their work in Hammond and Steward (2008: 105–68).

Chapter 2

1 See Willett ([1978] 1986: 13–36) for a chronology of events, productions and publications pertaining to Piscator's life and work.

2 See Snyder (1966: 11–43) for a clear summary of events leading to the establishment of the Weimar Republic. The book usefully includes a set of readings that gathers historical materials such as the Treaty of Versailles and the Weimar Constitution, along with individual accounts, proclamations and manifesto statements.

3 See https://www.historytoday.com/archive/spartacist-uprising-berlin, accessed 11 November 2022, for a pithy thumbnail sketch of events.

4   See Rorrison's introduction to Piscator ([1929] 1980: chapter VIII, 85–90) for an account of the context leading up to *In Spite of Everything!*, and a list of scenes. Piscator's chapter entitled 'The Documentary Play' addresses his production (91–8). See Favorini (1995: xviii–xx) for a discussion of the production and its reception.

5   See Willett ([1978] 1986: 185–9) for a discussion of trajectories in the engagement of both Brecht and Piscator with the notion of 'epic theatre', and relations and differences between their work and writings in this respect. See also Willett (1970: 2–3) for a discussion of Piscator's impact on the work and thinking of Brecht. See also the sections entitled 'The Augsburger's Relationship to Piscator' and 'Piscator's Theatre' in Brecht (2014: ebook 15.183–6; and 15.189–91). Hoffmann notes that Piscator favoured an idea of epic theatre that was educational and focused on relations between the individual and society, but was nonetheless distinct from Brecht's conception (Hoffmann 1970: 25). See also Arjomand (2018: 98–9) for a discussion of differences between the approach of the two directors. For Brecht's writings on theatre, see Brecht (2014; 2015). The former presents a collation of Brecht's *Messingkauf Dialogues* (here entitled *Buying Brass*, a literal translation of the German), along with a set of 'modelbooks' – production notes and templates – relating to specific plays and productions; the latter is an expanded and updated version of the celebrated collection of writings edited by John Willett (originally published in 1964).

6   For reflections on the Living Newspaper project, see Cobb (1990) and Goldman (1973). As an aside concerning historical congruence, it's worth noting that in 1938 (two years after the production of *Triple-A Plowed Under*) *Busmen* was presented by London Unity Theatre as a Living Newspaper production, with a script overseen by John Allen.

7   See Levi and Rothberg (2003: 273–4), for a brief discussion of subsequent shifts in Adorno's thinking towards an acknowledgement of the place and need for art that responds to suffering.

Chapter 3

1. For reference to dissenting views concerning Smith's work of representation – for example, arguing that she does not sufficiently address some constituencies nor reveal her own position – see Weatherston (2008: 193) and Forsyth (2009: 143).

2. See Baldassare ([1994] 2019) for reflections upon various aspects of the incident and its aftermath. For a timeline of the Rodney King beating and subsequent trial and riots, see Smith (1994: 257–65).

3. For a production history of *Twilight: Los Angeles, 1992*, see Smith (1994: xxvii–xxviii). See Weatherston (2008: 196–200) for an account of Smith's process in making the production, and 199 for an outline of the background of the dramaturgs. As Bernstein notes, 'no definitive text of the play exists ... of the 53 pieces Smith performed in the production at the Ford Theatre in Washington, D.C. in 1997, fewer than half appeared in the published "script"' (2000: 123). A film adaptation of the play, written by Smith and directed by Marc Levin, was shown at the Sundance Film Festival, 2000, and broadcast on PBS as part of the 'Stage on Screen' series, 29 April 2001. See Forsyth (2009: 147–8) for a discussion of compositional and tonal differences between *Fires in the Mirror* and *Twilight*.

4. See Brittain et al. (2014: 294–8) for a chronology of events, from the stabbing of Stephen Lawrence on 22 April 1993 to the submission of the Kent Report (a report by the Police Complaints Authority) to the Home Secretary, Jack Straw, in December 1997. As might be expected given the nature of this case, Wikipedia in this instance provides a clear and well-referenced account. See https://en.wikipedia.org/wiki/Murder_of_Stephen_Lawrence (accessed 28 January 2023).

5. The production ran at the Tricycle Theatre from 12 January to 6 February 1999. It played at the Theatre Royal Stratford East (16 to 27 February), the Victoria Palace Theatre, London (3 to13 March) and the Lyttelton Theatre, Royal National Theatre (21 to 25 Sept), along with a national tour. A televised version of the theatre show, directed by Kent and produced by the

BBC, was broadcast on BBC2 on 21 February 1999. Separately, a TV drama, *The Murder of Stephen Lawrence*, written and directed by Paul Greengrass, produced by Mark Redhead, was broadcast on ITV on 8 February 1999. The production won the 2000 British Academy of Film and Television Award (BAFTA) for Best Single TV Drama. A three-part sequel entitled *Stephen*, written by Frank Cottrell-Boyce and Joe Cottrell-Boyce, directed by Alrick Riley and produced by HTM Television, was broadcast on ITV between 30 August and 13 September 2021.

6 Kent was artistic director of the Tricycle Theatre from 1984 to 2012. For a history of the Tricycle Theatre, focusing on Kent's tenure as artistic director, see Stoller (2013).

7 See Morosetti and Okagbue 2021: 'Introduction', Note 9 for a list of volumes published from 1998 to 2014 on relations between race and theatre.

Chapter 4

1 The first and second novels, *Wolf Hall* (2009) and *Bring up the Bodies* (2012), won the Booker Prize for their respective years of publication.

2 See Birgfeld et al. 2015, for an introduction to the company and an account of the scope and success of its work. The company's website, https://www.rimini-protokoll.de/website/en/, contains extensive documentation concerning its respective projects.

3 *Radio Muezzin*, concept and direction by Stefan Kaegi, presented by Rimini Protokoll, try-out at El Sawy Culturewheel, Zamalek, Cairo, 5 December 2008; opened at Hebbel Am Ufer (HAU2), Berlin, 3–9 March 2009, various performances until 2012. For details of the project, see https://www.rimini-protokoll.de/website/en/project/radio-muezzin (accessed 20 August 2023). A video recording of the production is available on this webpage.

4 See the programme's website: https://www.thisamericanlife.org/about (accessed 2 January 2023).

5   *Serial* (Season 2) (2015–16) [podcast], produced by Sarah Koenig and Julie Snyder, US: *This American Life*. A comprehensive website for the programme includes each episode, with a listening guide, accompanying materials and transcripts. Available online: https://serialpodcast.org/season-two (accessed 2 January 2023).

6   Available online: https://serialpodcast.org/2015/12/season-two-welcome (accessed 2 January 2023).

7   *Serial* podcast, 'Transcript: Episode 02: The Golden Chicken', https://serialpodcast.org/season-two/2/the-golden-chicken/transcript (accessed 2 January 2023).

8   https://www.robinbrussels.be/about (accessed 5 January 2023).

9   https://bamaflexweb.hogent.be/BMFUIDetailxOLOD.aspx?a=102910&b=5&c=2 (accessed 5 January 2023).

10 See 'Domo de Eŭropa Historio en Ekzilo', https://www.robinbrussels.be/domo-de-e-ropa-historio-en-ekzilo (accessed 5 January 2023).

11 See https://www.mucem.org/en/domo-de-europa-historio-en-ekzilo (accessed 5 January 2023).

12 See https://www.thomasbellinck.com/counter-museum (accessed 6 January 2023).

13 See https://www.thomasbellinck.com/abc-6 (accessed 6 January 2023).

14 *The Wall*, dir. Juan Ayala, prod. and dramaturgy Miguel Oyarzun, was presented by Teatro de la Abadía and Tobacco Factory Theatres at Teatro de la Abadía, Madrid, 10–12 February 2023 and The Tobacco Factory, Bristol, 22–24 February 2023.

15 See https://ballhausnaunynstrasse.de/about/ (accessed 7 January 2023).

16 *Even at the Risk* was presented at the Ballhaus Naunynstrasse, Berlin, on 26 November 2022; and at the same venue on 7 and 8 January 2023 as part of the *Black Berlin Black Widerstand* [Resistance] Festival.

REFERENCES

Adorno, Theodor W. ([1967] 1981) *Prisms*, trans. Samuel and Shierry Weber, Cambridge, MA: The MIT Press.

Agamben, Giorgio (2009) *What is an Apparatus? And Other Essays*, trans. David Kishik and Stefan Pedatella, Stanford, CA: Stanford University Press.

Amine, Khalid (2009) 'Radio Muezzin: Al-adhan as a Public Affair', *Textures: Online Platform for Interweaving Performance Cultures*, 5 October 2009. Available online: https://www.textures-archiv.geisteswissenschaften.fu-berlin.de/index.html%3Fp=526.html (accessed 2 January 2023).

Anonymous (2009) 'The Muezzins' Call to the Stage', *The Irish Times*, 19 September 2009. Available online: https://www.irishtimes.com/news/the-muezzins-call-to-the-stage-1.741573 (accessed 29 December 2022).

Arjomand, Minou (2018) *Staged: Show Trials, Political Theater, and the Aesthetics of Judgment*, New York: Columbia University Press.

Baldassare, Mark ([1994] 2019) 'Introduction', in M. Baldassare (ed.), *The Los Angeles Riots: Lessons for the Urban Future*, New York and Abingdon: Routledge, 1–17.

Baron, Zach (2016) '*Serial* Season 2 Wasn't a Phenomenon—But it Was Still Pretty Phenomenal', *GQ*, 2 April 2016. Available online: https://www.gq.com/story/serial-season-2 (accessed 2 January 2023).

Bateman, John, Janina Wildfeuer and Tuomo Hiippala (2017) *Multimodality: Foundations, Research and Analysis: A Problem-Oriented Introduction*, Berlin and Boston: De Gruyter.

Becker, Lutz (1970) 'The German Proletarian Theatre and Erwin Piscator', in Ludwig Hoffmann (ed.), *Erwin Piscator: Political Theatre 1920–1966*, London: Arts Council of Great Britain, 13–20.

Bekiempis, V. (2023) '"I'm just trying to go home": Tyre Nichols Heard Pleading in Released Video', *The Guardian*, 28 January 2023. Available online: https://www.theguardian.com/us-news/2023/jan/27/tyre-nichols-video-memphis-police-footage-released (accessed 28 January 2023).

Bellinck, Thomas (2018) 'Thomas Bellinck – House of European History in Exile', EASTAP, 31 December 2018. Available online: https://eastap.com/2018/12/31/thomas-bellinck-house-of-european-history-in-exile/ (accessed 5 January 2023).

Bernstein, Robin (2000) 'Rodney King, Shifting Modes of Vision, and Anna Deavere Smith's *Twilight: Los Angeles, 1992*', *Journal of Dramatic Theory and Criticism*, 14:2, 121–34.

Birgfeld, Johannes, Ulrike Garde and Meg Mumford (2015), 'Introduction: Diverse and Close-Up Navigations of Rimini Protokoll's Theatre', in J. Birgfeld, U. Garde and M. Mumford (eds), *Rimini Protokoll Close-Up: Lektüren*, Hannover: Wehrhahn, ix–xxv.

Bishop, Claire (2012) 'Delegated Performance: Outsourcing Authenticity', *October*, 140, 91–112.

Boles, William C. (ed.) (2022) *Theater in a Post-Truth World: Text, Politics, and Performance*, London: Methuen Drama.

Brecht, Bertolt (2014) *Brecht on Performance: Messingkauf and Modelbooks*, edited by Tom Kuhn, Steve Giles and Marc Silberman, trans. Charlotte Ryland, Romy Fursland, Steve Giles, Tom Kuhn and John Willett, London: Bloomsbury, 2014.

Brecht, Bertolt (2015) *Brecht on Theatre*, edited by Marc Silberman, Steve Giles and Tom Kuhn, trans. Jack Davis, Romy Fursland, Steve Giles, Victoria Hill, Kristopher Imbrigotta, Marc Silberman and John Willett, London and New York: Bloomsbury.

Brewer, M. F., L. Goddard and D. Osborne (2015) 'Framing Black British Drama: Past to Present', in M. F. Brewer, L. Goddard and D. Osborne (eds), *Modern and Contemporary Black British Drama*, London: Palgrave, 1–14.

Briegleb, Till (2015) 'Between Theatre and Reality', *DE: Magazin Deutchland*, 3, 50–3.

Brittain, V., N. Kent, R. Norton-Taylor and G. Slovo (2014) *The Tricycle: Collected Tribunal Plays 1994–2012*, London: Oberon Books.

Carlson, Marvin (1996) 'Performing the Self', *Modern Drama*, 39:4, 599–608.

Casey, Louise (2023) *Baroness Casey Review: Final Report*, London: Metropolitan Police, March 2023. Available online: https://www.met.police.uk/SysSiteAssets/media/downloads/met/about-us/baroness-casey-review/update-march-2023/baroness-casey-review-march-2023a.pdf (accessed 22 August 2023).

Cathcart, Brian (2012) *The Case of Stephen Lawrence*, London: Penguin.
Cavendish, Richard (2009) 'The Spartacist Uprising in Berlin', *History Today*, 59:1. Available online: https://www.historytoday.com/archive/spartacist-uprising-berlin (accessed 11 November 2022).
Cobb, Gerry (1990) '"Injunction Granted" in its Times: A Living Newspaper Reappraised', *New Theatre Quarterly*, 6:23, 279–96.
Cohen, Sarah Blacher, and Joanne B. Koch (eds) (2007) *Shared Stages: Ten American Dramas of Blacks & Jews*, Albany: State University of New York Press.
D'Ancona, Matthew (2017) *Post Truth: The New War on Truth and How to Fight Back*, London: Ebury Press.
Dahl, Mary Karen (2009) 'Sacrificial Practices: Creating the Legacy of Stephen Lawrence', in Patrick Anderson and Jisha Menon (eds), *Violence Performed: Local Routes and Global Routes of Conflict*, Basingstoke: Palgrave Macmillan, 126–51.
Davenport, Mackenzie (2021) 'Katie Mitchell – Crafting Live Cinema', 2 July 2021. Available online: https://www.youtube.com/watch?v=GokvM33fJAc (accessed 13 August 2023).
Djonov, Emilia, and Sumin Zhao (2014) 'From Multimodal to Critical Multimodal Studies through Popular Discourse', in Emilia Djonov and Sumin Zhao (eds.), *Critical Multimodal Studies of Popular Discourse*, New York and London: Routledge, 1–14.
Favorini, Attilio (ed.) (1995) *Voicings: Ten Plays from the Documentary Theater*, Hopewell, NJ: The Ecco Press.
Feldman, Benedict Alexander (2021) 'The Theatre of Culpability: Reading the Tricycle's Plays through the Trial of Adolf Eichmann', *Law, Culture and the Humanities*, 17:3, 598–619.
Fernandes, Carla (2016) 'Introduction', in Carla Fernandes (ed.), *Multimodality and Performance*, Newcastle upon Tyne: Cambridge Scholars Publishing, 1–6.
Flood, Alison (2016) '"Post-truth" Named Word of the Year by Oxford Dictionaries', *The Guardian*, 15 November 2016. Available online: https://www.theguardian.com/books/2016/nov/15/post-truth-named-word-of-the-year-by-oxford-dictionaries (accessed 18 August 2023).
Flood, Alison (2017) 'Fake News is "Very Real" Word of the Year for 2017', *The Guardian*, 2 November 2017. Available online: https://

www.theguardian.com/books/2017/nov/02/fake-news-is-very-real-word-of-the-year-for-2017 (accessed 18 August 2023).

Forsyth, Alison (2009) 'Performing Trauma: Race Riots and beyond in the Work of Anna Deavere Smith', in Alison Forsyth and Chris Megson (eds), *Get Real: Documentary Theatre Past and Present*, London and New York: Palgrave Macmillan, 140–50.

Forsyth, Alison, and Chris Megson (2009) 'Introduction', in Alison Forsyth and Chris Megson (eds), *Get Real: Documentary Theatre Past and Present*, London and New York: Palgrave Macmillan, 1–5.

Fowler, Benjamin (2018) '(Re)Mediating the Modernist Novel: Katie Mitchell's Live Cinema Work', in Kara Reilly (ed), *Contemporary Approaches to Adaptation in Theatre*, London: Palgrave Macmillan, 97–119.

Garde, Ulrike, and Meg Mumford (2016) *Theatre of Real People: Diverse Encounters at Berlin's Hebbel am Ufer and Beyond*, London: Methuen Drama.

Gardner, Lyn (2009) 'How Real is Reality Theatre?', *The Guardian*, 13 October 2009. Available online: https://www.theguardian.com/stage/theatreblog/2009/oct/11/reality-verbatim-theatre (accessed 29 December 2022).

Goddard, L. (2015) *Contemporary Black British Playwrights: Margins to Mainstream*, Basingstoke: Palgrave Macmillan.

Goldman, Arnold (1973) 'Life and Death of the Living Newspaper Unit', *Theatre Quarterly*, 3:9, 69–82.

Gordon, Mel (1974) 'Dada Berlin: A History of Performance (1918–1920)', *The Drama Review*, 18:2, 114–24.

Greene, Steve (2018) '"Serial" Season 2 Is Better than You Remember and an Unexpected Time Capsule Worth Revisiting', *IndieWire*, 18 September 2018. Available online: https://www.indiewire.com/2018/09/serial-season-2-bowe-bergdahl-podcast-revisiting-1202004946/ (accessed 2 January 2023).

Gropius, Walter (1970) 'Erwin Piscator', in Ludwig Hoffmann (ed.), *Erwin Piscator: Political Theatre 1920–1966*, London: Arts Council of Great Britain, 35–6.

Hamilton, Margaret (2015) '"Make a Map, Not a Tracing": Disclosing the Cartographic Aesthetic of Rimini Protokoll', in J. Birgfeld, U. Garde and M. Mumford (eds), *Rimini Protokoll Close-Up: Lektüren*, Hannover: Wehrhahn, 73–91.

Hammond, Will, and Dan Steward (eds) (2008) *Verbatim, Verbatim: Contemporary Documentary Theatre*, London: Oberon Books.

Hernández, Paola (2021) *Staging Lives in Latin American Theatre*, Evanston, IL: Northwestern University Press.

Hill, Annette (2005) *Reality TV: Audiences and Popular Factual Television*, London: Routledge.

Hoffmann, Ludwig (ed.) (1970), *Erwin Piscator: Political Theatre 1920–1966*, Berlin and London: Deutsche Akademie der Künste zu Berlin/Arts Council of Great Britain.

Hutchinson, Pamela (2017) 'Where to Begin with City Symphonies', BFI, 1 September 2017. Available online: https://www2.bfi.org.uk/news-opinion/news-bfi/features/where-begin-city-symphonies (accessed 13 August 2023).

Hutchison, Yvette (2010) 'Post-1990s Verbatim Theatre in South Africa: Exploring an African Concept of "Truth"', in Carol Martin (ed.), *Dramaturgy of the Real on the World Stage*, London: Palgrave Macmillan, 61–71.

Irmer, Thomas (2006) 'A Search for New Realities: Documentary Theatre in Germany', *The Drama Review*, 50:3 (T191), 16–28.

Jacobson, Kelsey (2023) *Real-ish: Audiences, Feeling, and the Production of Realness in Contemporary Performance*, Montreal: McGill-Queen's University Press.

Jewitt, Carey ([2009] 2014) 'An Introduction to Multimodality', in Carey Jewitt (ed.), *The Routledge Handbook of Multimodal Analysis*, London and New York: Routledge, 15–30.

Kanelo-Lucas, Valerie Kaneko (2007) '"There's No Justice – Just Us": Black Britons, British Asians, and the Criminal Justice System in Verbatim Drama', in R. Victoria Arana (ed.), *'Black' British Aesthetics Today*, Newcastle: Cambridge Scholars Press, 262–82.

Khan, Hassan (2009) 'Radio Muezzin'. Available online: https://www.bidoun.org/articles/radio-muezzin (accessed 28 December 2022).

Koenig, Sarah (2016) 'Was Anyone Killed Looking for Bowe Bergdahl? Some Hard Evidence, at Long Last', Serial, 10 June 2016. Available online: https://serialpodcast.org/posts/2016/10/was-anyone-killed-looking-for-bowe-bergdahl-some-hard-evidence-at-long-last (accessed 2 January 2022).

Kondo, Dorinne (2000) '(Re)visions of Race: Contemporary Race Theory and the Cultural Politics of Racial Crossover in Documentary Theatre', *Theatre Journal*, 52:1, 81–107.

Kress, Gunter ([2009] 2014) 'What is Mode?', in Carey Jewitt (ed.), *The Routledge Handbook of Multimodal Analysis*, London and New York: Routledge, 60–75.

Kushner, Tony ([1992] 2007) *Angels in America: A Gay Fantasia on National Themes. Part One: Millennium Approaches. Part Two: Perestroika*, London: Nick Hern Books.

Ledger, Adam J. (2018) '"The Thrill of Doing it Live": Devising and Performing Katie Mitchell's International "Live Cinema" Productions', in Kara Reilly (ed.), *Contemporary Approaches to Adaptation in Theatre*, London: Palgrave Macmillan, 69–90.

Lehmann, Hans-Thies ([1999] 2006) *Postdramatic Theatre*, trans. Karen Jürs-Munby, Oxford and New York: Routledge.

Levi, Neil and Michael Rothberg (2003) 'Literature and Culture after Auschwitz: Introduction', in N. Levi and M. Rothberg (eds), *The Holocaust: Theoretical Readings*, Edinburgh: Edinburgh University Press, 273–6.

Ley-Piscator, Maria (1967) *The Piscator Experiment: The Political Theatre*, New York: Heineman.

Locker, Melissa (2016) '*Serial* Season Two: Why Did the "Must-listen Show" Suffer a Sophomore Slump?', *The Guardian*, 5 April 2016. Available online: https://www.theguardian.com/tv-and-radio/2016/apr/05/serial-season-two-bowe-bergdahl-podcast (accessed 2 January 2023).

Luckhurst, Mary (2008) 'Verbatim Theatre, Media Relations and Ethics', in Nadine Holdsworth and Mary Luckhurst (eds), *A Concise Companion to Contemporary British and Irish Drama*, Oxford: Blackwell Publishing, 200–22.

Macpherson, W. (1999) *The Stephen Lawrence Inquiry: Report of an Inquiry by Sir William Macpherson of Cluny*, London: United Kingdom Government. Available online: https://assets.publishing.service.gov.uk/government/uploads/system/uploads/attachment_data/file/277111/4262.pdf (accessed 18 April 2023).

Magris, Erica, and Béatrice Picon-Vallin (2019) *Les théâtres documentaires*, Lacoste: Deuxieme Epoque.

Malina, Judith (2012) *The Piscator Notebook*, London and New York: Routledge.

Malzacher, Florian (2015) 'Introduction', in steirischer herbst and Florian Malzacher (eds), *Truth is Concrete: A Handbook for Artistic Strategies in Real Politics*, Berlin: Sternberg Press, 5–11.

Mantel, Hilary (2009) *Wolf Hall*, London: Fourth Estate.

Mantel, Hilary (2012) *Bring Up the Bodies*, London: Fourth Estate.

Mantel, Hilary (2020) *The Mirror and the Light*, London: Fourth Estate.
Marlow, A. and Loveday, B. (2000) 'Race, Policing and the Need for Leadership', in A. Marlow and B. Loveday (eds), *After Macpherson: Policing after the Stephen Lawrence Inquiry*, Lyme Regis: Russell House Publishing, 1–3.
Martin, Carol (2006) 'Bodies of Evidence', *The Drama Review*, 50:3 (T191), 8–15.
Martin, Carol (2010) 'Introduction: Dramaturgy of the Real', in Carol Martin (ed.), *Dramaturgy of the Real on the World Stage*, London: Palgrave Macmillan, 1–14.
Martin, Carol (2013) *Theatre of the Real*, Basingstoke: Palgrave Macmillan.
Mason, Gregory (1977) 'Documentary Drama from the Revue to the Tribunal', *Modern Drama*, 20:3, 263–77.
McGrath, Melanie (2007) *The Long Exile: A Tale of Inuit Betrayal and Survival in the High Arctic*, New York: Alfred A. Knopf.
McIntyre, Lee (2018) *Post-Truth*, Cambridge, MA: MIT Press.
Morosetti, T. and Okagbue, O. (eds) (2021) *The Palgrave Handbook of Theatre and Race*, Basingstoke: Palgrave Macmillan.
Mroué, Rabih (2015) 'Facts and Fiction', in steirischer herbst and Florian Malzacher (eds), *Truth is Concrete: A Handbook for Artistic Strategies in Real Politics*, Belin: Sternberg Press, 164–6.
Mülhausen, Walter (2015) 'Social Democratic Party of Germany (SDP)', *International Encyclopedia of the First World War*, 18 December 2015. Available online: https://encyclopedia.1914-1918-online.net/article/social_democratic_party_of_germany_spd (accessed 29 October 2022).
Murray-Brown, Jeremy (2003) 'Documentary Films', in the *Encyclopedia of International Media and Communication*, San Diego: The Academic Press. Available online: https://www.bu.edu/jeremymb/files/2017/07/encyclopedia-entry-copy-pdf.pdf (accessed 18 August 2023).
Nanook of the North (1922) [film] dir. Robert Flaherty, US: Pathé Exchange. Available online: https://www.youtube.com/watch?v=lkW14Lu1IBo (accessed 13 August 2023).
Nashawaty, Chris (2016) '"Serial" Season 2 finale recap: "Present for Duty"', *Entertainment*, 1 April 2016. Available online: https://ew.com/article/2016/04/01/serial-season-2-finale-recap-bowe-bergdahl/ (accessed 2 January 2023).

NEH (2015) 'Anna Deavere Smith: Jefferson Lecture 2015', National Endowment for the Humanities. Available online: https://www.neh.gov/about/awards/jefferson-lecture/anna-deavere-smith-biography (accessed 11 April 2023).

Norton-Taylor, Richard (2003) 'Courtroom Drama', *The Guardian*, 4 November 2003. Available online: https://www.theguardian.com/stage/2003/nov/04/theatre.politicsandthearts (accessed 15 August 2023).

Norton-Taylor, Richard (2014) *The Colour of Justice. Based on the Transcripts of the Stephen Lawrence Inquiry*, in V. Brittain, N. Kent, R. Norton-Taylor and G. Slovo, *The Tricycle: Collected Tribunal Plays 1994–2012*, London: Oberon Books, 291–415.

Paget, Derek (1987) '"Verbatim Theatre": Oral History and Documentary Techniques', *New Theatre Quarterly*, 3:12, 317–36.

Paget, Derek (1990) *True Stories? Documentary Drama on Radio, Screen and Stage*, Manchester and New York: Manchester University Press.

Paget, Derek (1998) *No Other Way to Tell it: Dramadoc/Documdrama on Television*, Manchester and New York: Manchester University Press.

Paget, Derek (2009) 'The "Broken Tradition" of Documentary Theatre and its Continued Powers of Endurance', in Alison Forsyth and Chris Megson (eds), *Get Real: Documentary Theatre Past and Present*, London and New York: Palgrave Macmillan, 224–38.

Paterson, Eddie (2015) *The Contemporary American Monologue: Performance and Politics*, London: Bloomsbury.

Peacock, K. D. (2015) 'The Social and Political Context of Black British Theatre: The 2000s', in M. F. Brewer, L. Goddard, and D. Osborne (eds), *Modern and Contemporary Black British Drama*, London: Palgrave, 147–60.

Peters, Sarah (2017) 'The Function of Verbatim Theatre Conventions in Three Australian Plays', *NJ (Drama Australia Journal)*, 41:2, 117–26.

Pickering, Kenneth, and Jayne Thompson (2013) *Naturalism in Theatre: Its Development and Legacy*, Basingstoke: Palgrave Macmillan.

Piscator, Erwin ([1929] 1980), *The Political Theatre*, trans. Hugh Rorrison, London: Eyre Methuen.

Piscator, Erwin, and Felix Gasbarra (1995) *In Spite of Everything!*, trans. Richard Korb with Attilio Favorini, in A. Favorini (ed.), *Voicings: Ten Plays from the Documentary Theater*, Hopewell, NJ: The Ecco Press, 1995, 1–7.

Radosavljević, Duška (2013) *Theatre-Making: Interplay between Text and Performance in the 21st Century*, Basingstoke: Palgrave Macmillan.

Rau, Milo (2018) 'Ghent Manifesto', in Milo Rau, *Global Realism: Golden Book I*, trans. Lily Climenhaga, Berlin: NTGent/Verbrecher Verlag, 279–81.

Rebellato, Dan (2010) 'Introduction: Naturalism and Symbolism: Early Modernist Practice', in Maggie B. Gale and John F. Deeney (eds), *Routledge Drama Anthology and Sourcebook: From Modernism to Contemporary Performance*, Abingdon: Routledge, 6–24.

Rees, Catherine (2019) *Contemporary British Drama*, London: Bloomsbury.

Reinelt, Janelle (1996) 'Performing Race: Anna Deavere Smith's Fires in the Mirror', *Modern Drama*, 39:4, 609–17.

Reinelt, Janelle (2009) 'The Promise of Documentary', in Alison Forsyth and Chris Megson (eds), *Get Real: Documentary Theatre Past and Present*, Basingstoke: Palgrave Macmillan, 6–23.

Renov, Michael (1993) 'Introduction: The Truth about Non-Fiction', in Michael Renov (ed.), *Theorizing Documentary*, New York and London: Routledge, 1–11.

Roose, Kevin (2021) 'What is QAnon, the Viral Pro-Trump Conspiracy Theory?', *The New York Times*, 3 September 2021. Available online: https://www.nytimes.com/article/what-is-qanon.html (accessed 14 August 2023).

Roscoe, Jane, and Craig Hight (2001) *Faking it: Mock Documentary and the Subversion of Factuality*, Manchester: Manchester University Press.

Rotha, Paul (1980) 'Nanook and the North', *Studies in Visual Communication*, 6:2, 33–60.

Rothman, William (1997) *Documentary Film Classics*, Cambridge: Cambridge University Press.

Schneider, Rebecca (2011) *Performing Remains: Art and War in Times of Theatrical Reenactment*, London: Routledge.

Schulze, Daniel (2017) *Authenticity in Contemporary Theatre and Performance: Make it Real*, London: Methuen Drama.

Serial Productions (2022), '"Serial": Season 2', 20 September 2022. Available online: https://www.nytimes.com/2022/09/20/podcasts/serial-season-2.html (accessed 2 January 2023).

Shapiro, Edward S. (2006) *Crown Heights: Blacks, Jews, and the 1991 Brooklyn Riot*, Waltham, MA: Brandeis University Press.

Smith, Anna Deavere (n.d.) 'How Do You Get into Character?', *Big Think*. Available online: https://www.youtube.com/watch?v=NkjADgWRq3Y, accessed 11 February 2023.

Smith, Anna Deavere (1994) *Twilight – Los Angeles, 1992: On the Road: A Search for American Character*, New York: Anchor Books.

Smith, Anna Deavere (2007) *Fires in the Mirror*, in Sarah Blacher Cohen and Joanne B. Koch (eds), *Shared Stages: Ten American Dramas of Blacks & Jews*, Albany: State University of New York Press, 465–542.

Smith, Cherise (2011) *Enacting Others: Politics of Identity in Eleanor Antin, Nikki S. Lee, Adrian Piper, and Anna Deavere Smith*, Durham, NC and London: Duke University Press.

Snyder, Louis L. (1966) *The Weimar Republic: A History of Germany from Ebert to Hitler*, New York: Van Nostrand.

Sowińska, Agnieszka (2010) 'Reality from the Bottom Up: Documentary Theatre in Poland', in Carol Martin (ed.), *Dramaturgy of the Real on the World Stage*, London: Palgrave Macmillan, 72–9.

Stoller, Terry (2013) *Tales of the Tricycle Theatre*, London and New York: Bloomsbury Methuen.

Taylor, Diana (2003) *The Archive and the Repertoire: Performing Cultural Memory in the Americas*, Durham, NC: Duke University Press.

Taylor, Lib (2013) 'Voice, Body and the Transmission of the Real in Documentary Theatre', *Contemporary Theatre Review*, 23:3, 368–79.

Taylor, Paul and Carlos Sanchez (1992) 'Bush Orders Troops into Los Angeles', *Washington Post*, 2 May 1992. Available online: https://www.washingtonpost.com/archive/politics/1992/05/02/bush-orders-troops-into-los-angeles/4c4711a6-f18c-41ed-b796-6a8a50d6120d/ (accessed 23 April 2023).

Terkel, Studs (1970) *Hard Times: An Oral History of the Great Depression*, London: Allen Lane The Penguin Press.

Thompson, Debby (2003) '"Is Race a Trope?": Anna Deavere Smith and the Question of Racial Performativity', *African American Review*, 37:1, 127–38.

Weatherston, Rosemary (2008) '"The True Words of Real People": Documenting the Myth of the Real in Anna Deavere Smith's Twilight: Los Angeles, 1992', *Ariel*, 39:1–2, 189–216.

Weiss, Peter ([1965[1995) *The Investigation*, in A. Favorini (ed.), *Voicings: Ten Plays from the Documentary Theater*, Hopewell, NJ: The Ecco Press, 44–139.

Wickstrom, Maurya (2018) *Fiery Temporalities in Theatre and Performance: The Initiation of History*, London: Methuen Drama.

Willet, John (1970), [No title], in Ludwig Hoffmann (ed.), *Erwin Piscator: Political Theatre 1920–1966*, Berlin and London: Deutsche Akademie der Künste zu Berlin/Arts Council of Great Britain, 2–12.

Willett, John ([1978] 1986) *The Theatre of Erwin Piscator: Half a Century of Politics in the Theatre*, London: Methuen.

Winstein-Hibbs, Sarah (2021) 'Staging Charisma: Anna Deavere Smith's Black Feminist Theater of the Multitude', *American Literary History*, 33:4, 800–22.

Winston, Brian (ed.) (2019) *The Documentary Film Book*, London: BFI/Bloomsbury Publishing.

Youker, Timothy (2018) *Documentary Vanguards in Modern Theatre*, Abingdon and New York: Routledge.

Žižek, Slavoj (2008) *Violence: Six Sideways Reflections*, London: Profile Books.

Zola, Émile (1893) *The Experimental Novel and Other Essays*, trans. Belle M. Sherman, New York: Cassell.

Zola, Émile ([1873] 2010) *Thérèse Raquin*, trans. Pip Broughton, in Maggie B. Gale and John F. Deeney (eds), *Routledge Drama Anthology and Sourcebook: From Modernism to Contemporary Performance*, Abingdon: Routledge, 25–50.

Zola, Émile ([1881] 2010) 'Naturalism in the Theatre', trans. Albert Bermel, in Maggie B. Gale and John F. Deeney (eds), *Routledge Drama Anthology and Sourcebook: From Modernism to Contemporary Performance*, Abingdon: Routledge, 126–37.

INDEX

actuality 71, 75, 147
  curated 86
  historical 108
  ideas/precepts of 11, 18, 151, 154
  and mediation/entertainment 117, 118, 136, 138, 154
  and 'news' 62
  and 'the repertoire' 14
  situations of the real 18
Adorno, Theodor 70, 71, 77
Agamben, Giorgio 31, 140
Amine, Khalid 121, 122, 127
Arendt, Hannah 104
Arjomand, Minou 35, 71, 72, 73, 81, 91, 154
Attenborough, David 3
apparatus (*dispositif*) 31, 140
Aukongo, Stefanie-Lahya 148, 149
authenticity 7, 12–14, 72, 87, 154
  authentic 28, 36, 39, 52, 68, 71, 83, 112
  authentication 4, 130, 139
  authenticity effects 13, 108
authorship 125, 153 (*see also* writing)
Ayala, Juan, *The Wall* (2022) 38, 144–7

Baldassare, Mark 88
Ballhaus Naunynstrasse 147–8
Baron, Zach 133
Bateman, John et al. 59
Bdawy, Hussein Gouda Hussein 121, 122, 128
Becker, Lutz 43, 61
Bellinck, Thomas
  Counter-Museum of Individual Freedoms 143
  Domo de Eŭropa Historio en Ekzilo (The House of European History in Exile) (2013–18) 38, 140–4
  overview of work 139–40
  Simple as ABC 144
Bergdahl, Bowe 131–8
Berlin – Symphony of a Big City (Cavalcanti and Ruttman, 1927) 22
Bernstein, Robin 82, 91
Bishop, Claire 27, 30
Black
  cultural positioning and performance 91, 148
  identity 85–6, 112, 149–50
  theatre/theatre-makers 110
Blank, Jessica, and Eric Jensen, *The Exonerated* (2000) 29
Blast Theory 30, 129
Blythe, Alecky 12 (*see also* Recorded Delivery)

Boles, William C., *Theater in a Post-Truth World* 11
Brecht, Bertolt 8
  and 'epic theatre' 59–61
  Messingkauf Dialogues 39
  on Erwin Piscator 42, 57, 60–1, 129
Briegleb, Till 129
Brooks, Duwayne 97, 98, 103

Carlson, Marvin 96
Casey Report, The 113
Cathcart, Brian 107
Cavendish, Richard 48
Cheeseman, Peter (*Hands Up – For You the War Is Ended!* [1971], *Fight for Shelton Bar!* [1974], *Miner Dig the Coal* [1981]) 26
Chekhov, Anton 16
Communist Party of Germany, see KPD
courtroom (drama/ characteristics) 105–7
cultural production
  developments in 11, 152
  fact-based 117–18
  in Germany 61
  both objective and subjective 117
  and repetition 34
  and 'truth' 2

D'Ancona, Matthew, *Post Truth: The New War on Truth and How to Fight Back* (2017) 115–16, 144, 150
Dada 42–3

Dahl, Mary Karen 104
Deavere Smith, Anna
  acting style 81–2
  Fires in the Mirror: Crown Heights Brooklyn and Other Identities (1992) 37, 83–8
  life and work 80–2
  'On the Road: A Search for American Character' 81
  Twilight: Los Angeles, 1992 (1993) 37, 83, 88–95
Die Rote Fahne (The Red Flag) 46
documentary/documentaries
  and the document 30–5, 54, 76–7, 144
  and experience 7–8, 76, 77, 82, 86, 89, 95, 138, 144
  and affect 92, 109
  and identity 80, 81, 150
  and film 26, 52, 56–7
  and news 62, 136
  and radio 26
  and reality 7, 22
  and representation 70–1, 126, 127, 129–30
  and storytelling (/narration) 62–3, 108, 133
  and technology 14–15, 22–3, 152
  and time 5, 93–4, 106–7, 108–9, 146–7
  and television 3, 26–7
documentary theatre
  characteristics 151–5
  conceptual framework 49–50

drama documentary 27
Dramatic Workshop, The 36, 67–9

Ebert, Friedrich 46, 47, 49, 51, 52
Edgar, David 106
Eisenstein, Sergei 56
Eisner, Kurt 48
entertainment 61, 136, 138
　format 2, 34, 117, 118, 130, 134
Evans, Walker 19–20
Even at the Risk (2023) 38, 148, 149–50
experimental theatre studios 61–2

'fake news' 9–10, 116
Favorini, Attilio 44, 45, 66
Federal Theatre Project 27, 66
Feldman, Benedict 104
female performance 91, 96, 149–50
Flaherty, Robert
　Moana (1926) 22
　Nanook of the North (1922) 18–21, 22
Flanagan, Hallie 66
Floyd, George 35
Forsyth, Alison, and Chris Megson, *Get Real* (2013) 24, 151
Foucault, Michel 31, 140
Franko B 28
Frazier, Darnella 35

Garde, Ulrike, and Meg Mumford, *Theatre of Real People* (2016) 13

Gardner, Lyn 125
Gasbarra, Felix 44
Germany
　historical account, 1914–19 46–9
　theatre structure and culture 58, 61
Goddard, Lynette 110
Greene, Steve 138
Gropius, Walter 57
Grotowski, Jerzy, *Akropolis* (1965) 12

Hamilton, Margaret 124, 125–6
Hare, David (*The Permanent Way* [2003], *Stuff Happens* [2004], *The Power of Yes* [2009]) 29
Hémêfa, Melanelle, B. C. 148, 149
Hindawy, Abdelmoty Abdelsamia Ali 121, 122, 123
Holliday, George 35, 88
Hutton Inquiry, The 28

Ibsen, Henrik 16
Immersive (theatre/experience) 58, 117, 129, 140
Irmer, Thomas 27

Jacobson, Kelsey, *Real-ish* 9, 116
journalist/ic 96, 135, 137, 138

Kaegi, Stefan 38, 119, 120–1, 124, 125, 127, 130
Kaneko-Lucas, Valerie 105, 106, 110

Kaufamn, Moises, *The Laramie Project* (2000) 28–9
Khan, Hassan 126, 127
Kent, Nicolas 28, 100, 101, 106, 109, 110
King, Rodney 35, 88, 89, 94, 114
Koenig, Sarah 131
  Serial (2014–18) 38, 130–2, 138–9
  Serial Season 2 (2015–16) 131–8
Kondo, Dorinne 91
KPD (*Kommunistische Partei Deutschlands*) 44, 47, 54, 62
Kress, Gunter 59
Kroesinger, Hans-Werner 27
Kushner, Tony, *Angels in America* (1991) 87

Lawrence, Doreen 112
Lawrence, Neville 111–12
Lawrence, Stephen 97, 109, 110
  The Stephen Lawrence case (context) 97–100
Lawson, Edmund (QC) 102, 103, 109
Lehmann, Hans-Thies
  Postdramatic Theatre ([1999] 2006) 42
Ley-Piscator, Maria 65–6, 67
Liebknecht, Karl 5, 36, 44, 51, 62
  and historical events 46–7, 49
  Liebknecht narrative in *In Spite of Everything!* 52–3
Littlewood, Joan
  Oh What a Lovely War! (Theatre Workshop, 1963) 26

Living Newspaper 27, 36, 66
  Triple-A Plowed Under (1936) 66
Living Theatre 37
Locker, Melissa 132
Losey, Joseph 66–7
Lucão, Ana 148, 149
Luxemburg, Rosa 46, 49, 53, 62

MacPherson, William (Sir) 97, 109
  Macpherson Inquiry/Report, The 97, 98–100, 107, 112, 113
Malina, Judith 37, 67
  on Piscator's approach 67, 74–5
Malzacher, Florian 8
The Mandalorian (2019) 18
Mansfield, Michael (QC) 103–4, 107, 109, 111
Martin, Carol
  documentary theatre characteristics 14, 152
  Theatre of the Real (2013) 24
Mantel, Hilary (*Wolf Hall* trilogy) 117–18
Mass-Observation 26
McIntyre, Lee, *Post-Truth* (2018) 10
Mitchell, Katie (and 'live cinema') 23
monologue performance 95–6
Mroué, Rabih 13
multimedia 2, 57–8
multimodality 58–9

Namous, Mansour Abdelsalam Mansour 121, 122, 123
Nashawaty, Chris 132

New School, The 67
Nichols, Tyre 114
non-actors/performers 30, 128–30, 145
Norton-Taylor, Richard 101, 106, 109
　Half the Picture (with John McGrath, 1993) 28, 32, 100, 101
　Justifying War (2003) 28
　The Colour of Justice: The Stephen Lawrence Enquiry (1999) 37, 97
　　production 100–12
　　theatrical style 104–9

Obama, Barack (President) 83, 115, 133
Orlan 28

Paget, Derek 11, 23, 24, 25–6, 32, 157 n.4
　definition of 'verbatim theatre' 25
Papke, Josephine 148
Paterson, Eddie 96
Piscator, Erwin 1, 27, 39, 41, 129, 154
　Burning Bush, The (1979) 72
　Flags (1923) 56, 63
　In Spite of Everything! 5, 36, 41, 42–5, 47, 50–65, 75–6, 88, 149–50
　　and epic theatre 60
　　multimodality 59
　　performances 63–5
　　play/text 49–54
　　scenography 54
　　storytelling and dramatic structure 62–3
　　use of film 56–7
　Investigation, The (see also Weiss, Peter) 72–5
　life and work 42–5
　The Political Theatre (1929) 36
　The Red Riot Revue (1924) 43
　S218 (1929) 72
　in the USA 65–9
　in the USSR 65
　in West Germany 69–75
podcasting 132
political theatre 29, 102
Pollesch, Rene 42
'post–truth' 9, 115–17, 144
postmodern/ism 10, 95, 116–17
punchdrunk 129
　The Drowned Man (2013) 18

QAnon 8–9

racism (and resistance) 79, 88, 109–12
　institutional 99, 113
Radosavljević, Duška 30, 34
Rau, Milo 1, 154
realism, the 'real', reality effect 18, 33, 77, 138, 153, 154
　de-real(ing) 139, 151
　reality trend 102, 119, 152
　theatres of the real 137
reality TV 27
Rebellato, Dan 16, 157 n.4
Recorded Delivery
　Come Out Eli (2003), *Cruising* (2006), *The*

Girlfriend Experience (2008) *Do We Look Like Refugees* (2010) 12
The Girlfriend Experience (2008) 29
Rees, Catherine 104
Reinelt, Janelle 38–9, 82
Renov, Michael 151
reportage 100, 118, 130, 136–8, 150
revelation 8, 15, 84, 107, 108, 117
  and the camera 23
  and intervention 6, 76, 146, 147
  process of 32
  and reality drive 120
Rimini Protokoll 28, 30, 42
  Annual Shareholder's Meeting (2008) 119
  approach 119–20
  Cargo Sofia-X (2008) 120, 121
  'experts of the everyday' 128, 130 (*see also* non-actors)
  100% City (2008) 128
  Radio Muezzin (2008) 38, 120–8
    and technology 124–5
  Situation Rooms (2013) 128
  World Climate Change Conference (2014/15) 119
Rorrison, Hugh 43, 61–2
Russian Revolution 48

Scarman Report, The (1981) 99
Scheidemann, Philipp 47
Schneider, Rebecca 5, 32, 33, 34, 151
Scott Inquiry ('Arms to Iraq') 28
set (scenography) 54, 74–5, 105–6
She She Pop 30, 42
Sherwood, Robert E. 20, 21
Slovo, Gillan 106
Smith, Cherise 95
Soans, Robin, *Talking to Terrorists* (2005) 9
Social Democratic Party of German, *see* SPD
social media 35, 117, 118, 136, 147
Snyder, Louis 48, 49
Spartacus Group/League/Spartacists 46, 47
SPD (*Sozialdemokratische Partei Deutschlands*) 46, 47, 49
Stoller 105, 110
Straw, Jack 98, 112
Strindberg, August 16
subjectification 31

Taylor, Diana 14, 32
Taylor, Lib 12
Terkel, Studs 95
  Hard Times: An Oral History of the Great Depression (1970) 27
This American Life 130
tribunal theatre 72, 104, 108–9
Tricycle Theatre 28
  and 'Tribunal' series 100–2
  and diversity 109–10
Trump, Donald 10
  inauguration 115–16

truth (notion of) 2, 7, 8–14, 154
TRVANIA 148, 149

Vaccari and Chadwick 9
Veiel, Andres 28
verbatim theatre 25, 29, 72, 104, 112–13, 153
Verhoeven, Dries 30
Vertov, Dziga
    Man with a Movie Camera (1929) 21–2, 32

Weatherston, Rosemary 96
Weiss, Peter
    The Investigation (1965) 37, 69–75, 76–7, 102
    'Fourteen Propositions for a Documentary Theatre' 71–2

Willett, John 58, 60
The Wooster Group, *Poor Theatre* (2004) 12
writing 32, 71, 80, 118, 137
    (*see also* authorship)
    playwriting 17

Youker, Timothy 25

Zetkin, Clara 46
Žižek, Slavoj 70, 71
Zola, Émile
    'The Experimental Novel' (1880) 15
    and Naturalism 16, 17, 18
    'Naturalism in the Theatre' (1881) 15
    and the scientific method 15–16
    Thérèse Raquin 16, 17, 18